"Someone's outside."

"What do we do?" Brenda asked Max.

"You wait here. But stay alert. I'll take Gus and check outside. Gus, seek." The animal darted out of the room.

Brenda stared nervously after them. How could Earl and Jed have found them here? She crossed to close the door, and an icy breeze blew her hair. Gasping, she turned toward the window as the tall, lanky man—the one called Jed—was climbing into the room, one hand outstretched toward her sleeping child.

"Maxwell! Help!" She dived toward the bed and threw her body on top of Rose.

A flying ball of fur hurdled through the air above her, and a piercing scream followed. Opening her eyes, she saw Gus, his teeth clamped into the man's arm.

"Go! Take Rose and hide," Maxwell commanded.

Brenda scrambled off the bed, clutching a sobbing Rose to her chest, and stumbled out of the room. She raced into the bathroom, closed and locked the door behind her. For the second time that night, she prayed no bullets would hit her and her daughter.

Rhonda Starnes is a retired middle-school language arts teacher who dreamed of being a published author from the time she was in seventh grade and wrote her first short story. She lives in North Alabama with her husband, whom she lovingly refers to as Mountain Man. They enjoy traveling and spending time with their children and grandchildren. Rhonda writes heart-and-soul suspense with rugged heroes and feisty heroines.

Books by Rhonda Starnes

Love Inspired Suspense

Rocky Mountain Revenge
Perilous Wilderness Escape
Tracked Through the Mountains
Abducted at Christmas
Uncovering Colorado Secrets
Cold Case Mountain Murder
Smoky Mountain Escape
In a Killer's Crosshairs
Ambushed in the Night

Visit the Author Profile page at LoveInspired.com.

AMBUSHED IN THE NIGHT

RHONDA STARNES

LOVE INSPIRED SUSPENSE
INSPIRATIONAL ROMANCE

If you purchased this book without a cover you should be aware that this book is stolen property. It was reported as "unsold and destroyed" to the publisher, and neither the author nor the publisher has received any payment for this "stripped book."

LOVE INSPIRED® SUSPENSE
INSPIRATIONAL ROMANCE

ISBN-13: 978-1-335-90652-6

Ambushed in the Night

Copyright © 2026 by Rhonda L. Starnes

All rights reserved. No part of this book may be used or reproduced in any manner whatsoever without written permission.

Without limiting the exclusive rights of any author, contributor or the publisher of this publication, any unauthorized use of this publication to train generative artificial intelligence (AI) technologies is expressly prohibited. Harlequin also exercises their rights under Article 4(3) of the Digital Single Market Directive 2019/790 and expressly reserves this publication from the text and data mining exception.

This is a work of fiction. Names, characters, places and incidents are either the product of the author's imagination or are used fictitiously. Any resemblance to actual persons, living or dead, businesses, companies, events or locales is entirely coincidental.

For questions and comments about the quality of this book, please contact us at CustomerService@Harlequin.com.

® is a trademark of Harlequin Enterprises ULC.

Love Inspired	HarperCollins Publishers
22 Adelaide St. West, 41st Floor	Macken House, 39/40 Mayor Street Upper,
Toronto, Ontario M5H 4E3, Canada	Dublin 1, D01 C9W8, Ireland
www.LoveInspired.com	www.HarperCollins.com

Printed in U.S.A.

Recycling programs for this product may not exist in your area

Blessed is the man that trusteth in the Lord,
and whose hope the Lord is.
—*Jeremiah* 17:7

For my father-in-law, Bobby.
Thank you for always reading my books.
I love you, PaPa.

ONE

Susan Warner picked up the snowman mug filled with hot cocoa, lifted it to her nose and inhaled deeply. The chocolate scent instantly soothed her jagged nerves. Indulging in a sweet treat had become her favorite way to end the day. Thankfully, her twenty-two-month-old daughter, Rose, normally slept through the night, going to bed at eight each evening—allowing Susan time to tidy up and unwind before her own bedtime—and not waking until six or seven the next morning.

Placing the mug on the kitchen island, she crossed to the small alcove she'd turned into a play area for her toddler, picked up a stuffed frog off the floor and tossed it into the wicker basket she used in place of a toy box. Then she quickly straightened the rest of the area—dropping three more stuffed animals into the basket and placing a coloring book and chunky crayons onto a side table before shoving several board books onto the lower shelf of the bookcase. After Susan finished tidying up, she pushed her arms into the dark purple down parka she'd purchased for her first winter in Maine and plucked the fuzzy, multicolored throw blanket off the chair, tucking it under her arm. Then she grabbed the baby monitor and her mug of cocoa off the kitchen island and headed to the back patio. It didn't matter that it was a brisk twenty-three degrees outside, or that the local forecast had predicted six inches of snow to fall on the already frozen ground overnight. Spending quiet time in the wooden swing each evening, while looking at the stars in the Maine sky and praying, had become the one ritual that had kept her sane as she learned to be a single mom living twelve hundred miles from everything she'd ever known.

After the FBI discovered that her husband, Joe, and her brother, Larry, had been involved in a multistate drug ring, trafficking drugs out of their family-owned auto body shop, the US Marshals Service had approached her with the idea of being placed in the United States Federal Witness Protection Program. Even though she had not participated in Larry's and Joe's illegal activities, the authorities believed she might unknowingly have information that could lead them to the head of the drug ring, putting her and Rose in danger. She didn't truly believe her life or that of her baby was in danger, but she jumped at the idea because she needed to escape the nightmare she'd found herself living in.

As per the instructions of Marshal Ackerman when she and Rose had entered WITSEC, she had fought hard to push the memory of her previous life as far back into the recesses of her mind as possible. Thankfully—if one could be thankful for having their life upended—Rose had been a newborn when they were placed in WITSEC, so there were no memories for her daughter to forget.

For Susan, though, it had taken hard work to rewire her thinking. Her first six months in Maine, she had sat down each day and written herself an alternative history, using the backstory details Marshal Ackerman had provided for her as a story outline and filling in the gaps as if she were an author writing a book. Once she'd memorized the details of her new story, it had been easier to convince herself she *was* Susan Warner, a widowed mom focused on raising a happy, healthy little girl. She hadn't realized at the time she'd written the details of her new persona that Joe, who was serving a life sentence for murder and drug trafficking, would be murdered in prison eighteen months later, and she would indeed become a widow. Mourning the loss of her husband and the life they'd planned for a second time had caused small cracks in the wall she'd built around her memories, allowing them to seep out from time to time.

Normally, when the details of her past broke free from the dark recesses of her mind, she would pluck them out like weeds before they had a chance to take root. But tonight, Valentine's Day, on what would have been hers and Joe's eighth wedding anniversary, she couldn't shake the melancholy cloud that hovered over her like a looming storm. And she was, without a doubt, once again, Brenda Frye Granger. A small-town girl from North Carolina, who'd never dreamed of anything more than living in the Appalachian Mountains and raising kids who spent their time playing barefoot outside, catching fireflies and enjoying fresh country air.

Giving herself a mental shake to clear her mind, she stepped outside, pulled the door closed behind her and crossed the stone pavers to the swing using only the glow of the light from the kitchen window, preferring to leave the patio light off so its glare wouldn't interfere with her ability to see the stars. Maybe, just for tonight, she would allow herself to be Brenda, feeling the emotions and all that went with that part of her life. Then, tomorrow, she could go back to the fake persona she'd worked so hard to embrace.

Placing the baby monitor and her mug on the

small side table, Brenda settled onto the swing with one leg tucked under the other and the blanket wrapped around her shoulders. Then she picked up the mug and took a sip of the hot liquid while using the toe of her shoe to move the swing gently, backward and forward.

Mindlessly, she fiddled with the necklace Joe had commissioned for their sixth wedding anniversary—the last they'd spent together. The necklace was the only thing that she'd kept from her past, unable to part with it since her Grandmother Alice's broach had been used as its centerpiece. Joe had said his reasoning for having the brooch crafted into a necklace was so she could wear it, instead of leaving it tucked away in a jewelry box. And one day, she'd be able to pass it down to their daughter.

Her mind drifted back to the day of Rose's birth, in a small cabin in the woods of eastern Tennessee. A day that should have been the most joyous of Brenda's life had turned into a day of fear and disillusionment.

Days earlier, Joe had killed an employee who'd discovered his and Larry's illegal activities. Sheriff Heath Dalton, who'd been nearing the end of a camping trip, had witnessed Joe and Larry burying the body in the Great Smoky Mountains National Park—and eventually Joe had been captured and taken into custody. Not believing Joe was capable of murder and thinking it had to be a big misunderstanding, Brenda had allowed Larry to trick her into aiding him in kidnapping nurse Kayla Eldridge. He'd insisted the nurse was a friend of the sheriff's and would be able to convince him Joe was innocent. Looking back now, Brenda couldn't believe how naïve she'd been.

Larry had taken the nurse at gunpoint and driven her and Brenda to a cabin deep in the woods, where they waited for the sheriff. Fearing that her brother would kill the nurse, along with the sheriff, she'd tried to get Kayla to make a run for it when there was an opportunity. At that point, Brenda was in labor, and Kayla wouldn't leave her. If it hadn't been for Kayla's help, there was a very good chance neither mother nor child would have survived. Despite all that had not gone as planned in her life, Brenda knew she was blessed to be alive, to have a daughter who was healthy and thriving and to live in a beautiful part of the country—even if it wasn't *home*.

"Dear Lord, forgive me for my mood today. I know every negative situation I have experienced has had an equal blessing. Where there has been darkness, You have provided Light." Looking heavenward, the stars gleaming like diamonds on black velvet, she smiled as she counted her blessings. "Moving with an infant, leaving all that I owned and all that I knew behind was difficult. Being able to live in a place where no one knows me and I've been able to heal emotionally, without fear of friends and neighbors pointing and whispering behind my back, has been a blessing. Suddenly becoming the sole caregiver for my daughter seemed bleak, but landing a work-from-home bookkeeping job that is flexible and allows me to keep Rose with me during the day instead of placing her in day care has been a true blessing. And finding a church home in my new community that has fed my soul and helped me deepen my relationship with You was more than I ever could have hoped for. Thank you for always providing for my needs even before I realize I have a need. I—"

"Check everywhere." A male voice came over the baby monitor.

Brenda froze. Was someone in her house? In Rose's room? She stopped the swing. With a shaking hand, she placed the mug on the side table, picked up the monitor and examined the video display.

Rose was asleep. She had kicked her cover off and wrapped her arm around her favorite stuffed animal—a kangaroo Brenda had bought her on their trip to the zoo to celebrate Rose's first birthday. All was quiet, except for a faint snore coming from her tiny daughter. Brenda released a breath. It must have been radio interference. Though it hadn't happened in all the months they'd lived in this house in Maine, it had happened once before, when Rose was only a few weeks old and they were in a safe house awaiting the official move.

She stretched to place the monitor back on the table and froze. A shadow crossed in front of Rose's bedroom door, briefly blocking the light from the hall.

"Find the woman while I search the rooms for the microchip. She won't be far. Not with the baby sleeping," the gruff male voice said.

"Yes, sir," a second male voice replied.

They *were* in her house! She had to get Rose out of there. Her eyes darted to the glass French door. Her cell phone lay on the kitchen island. Could she slip inside undetected? Not likely.

Her home was less than fourteen hundred square feet. They didn't know she was in the backyard, but it wouldn't take them long to find her. She stood, the swing swaying. Then she turned the volume of the baby monitor as low as she dared, desperate to hear the men's movements while praying they would leave Rose alone. Grabbing her mug, Brenda quickly darted across the backyard to the opposite corner of the house, thankful the snow hadn't fallen yet and her footsteps would not be obvious. She tossed the mug and the blanket behind an evergreen shrub, hiding any evidence that she had been there. Then she checked the baby monitor once more. Rose was still sleeping, and the men were nowhere in sight.

Brenda slipped the monitor into the pocket of her sweatpants. Now to get inside without being seen so she could get her gun and her baby. Pressing her hands against the house, she peeked in the window of the extra bedroom that she used as an office. A tall man with a beard, whom she did not recognize, pulled open a filing cabinet drawer, ruffled through the files and then slammed it shut. He was obviously not concerned about being heard or getting caught.

Reaching up with both hands, she jumped and grasped the top rail of the wooden fence that enclosed a small portion of the backyard, keeping out wild animals while providing a small, safe area for Rose to play outdoors. Using the balls of her feet, Brenda climbed three steps upward and then swung her right leg up and over. Stradling the top rail, she swung her left leg over and dropped to the ground with a soft thud. Now what? She was no longer trapped in the backyard, but she still needed to get to Rose. And Brenda's nearest neighbor was over a mile away...through the woods. Holding her breath and not moving a muscle, she listened.

The back door banged open. She peered through the small cracks between the horizontal wooden fence slats. A slender male figure walked to the edge of the patio and peered into the yard. Then he headed in her direction. Scooting away from the fence, she hid behind the large, square metal central air unit, removed the baby monitor from her pocket and turned the sound off. *Please, don't let him see me, Lord. And please, wrap Rose in a hedge of protection. Don't let them hurt my baby.*

"Jed, did you find her?" a man's voice asked from the other side of the fence.

Brenda squinted her eyes, concentrating on the small crack between the slats, and made out the shadow of the bearded man's head sticking through the window she'd peered through moments ago.

"No. She ain't out here," the lanky man, Jed, replied and turned away from the fence.

"She has to be outside somewhere. A mom will not leave her baby unattended."

"If you're so smart, you come look," Jed huffed. "There's no place for her to hide back here. Maybe she's out front."

"We would've seen her when we broke in," the bearded man reasoned. "The only places we haven't checked are the attic and the basement. You take the upstairs. I'll take the downstairs. We'll find her. Then we'll make her give us the microchip and shut her up, permanently."

"She can't be in the attic. The access ladder wasn't pulled down," Jed reasoned.

"Maybe the microchip is hidden up there. Search for it."

The sound of Jed running across the frozen ground echoed in the night. She stealthily climbed on top of the air unit and peered over the top of the fence just in time to see him disappear indoors. The bearded man was nowhere in sight, but he'd left the window open. *Thank You, Lord.*

She quickly swung over the fence and dropped into the backyard. Then she climbed through the open window. The sound of footsteps in the attic sent chills down her spine. She'd have to move stealthily or the bearded man in the basement would hear her footsteps the way she heard the ones coming from above.

Making her way across the hall and into her bedroom, she cautiously slid the closet door open, reached into the corner and withdrew the .22 rifle that Grandpa Henry—an elderly gentleman from church—had insisted on loaning her for protection. She kept the weapon loaded and ready. Then she crept to her daughter's room, propped the weapon against the dresser and grabbed the toddler carrier off the wooden peg by the door. Should she do a back or front carry? Rose preferred the back carry position, but that would mean as Brenda attempted to escape her child would be between her and the men with guns. Front carry it was.

She quickly put the carrier on and fastened all the snaps. Then, crossing to the crib, she picked up Rose and gently bounced her up and down. Whispering shushing sounds, Brenda slipped her—still sleeping—toddler into the carrier. Once Rose was secure, she draped a pink wool blanket over her tiny body, grasped the rifle by the barrel and headed for the door. After she reached her phone, she would slip outside, find a place to hide and call 911.

Tiptoeing down the hall, she pressed her back to the wall and inched her way past the ladder that the lanky man had pulled down from the ceiling to grant access to the attic.

"Stop! Earl, she's getting away!" Jed peered down at her, and a gun suddenly appeared in his hands.

She sprinted the last few feet down the hall and skidded around the corner just as a bullet hit the wall behind her. Footsteps clomped on the basement stairs as the other man raced up them. No time to grab her cell phone. She had to get out of there, fast.

Rose jerked awake and released a loud wail. Brenda threw open the front door, hurried down the porch steps and charged into the night.

"Shhh. Rose, it's okay. Mommy has you," she whispered urgently into her daughter's ear, but the child's wails grew louder. "Shhh. Let's play the quiet game."

Running into the woods bordering her property, Brenda prayed she could soothe her child so her cries weren't a beacon announcing their location. With no light to guide her way and the nearest neighbor a mile and a half away over treacherous terrain, she didn't know what would kill them first, the freezing temperature or the men with guns.

Maxwell Prescott pressed the power button on the remote and turned off the television. "Come on, Gus. Let's go to bed."

Gus, a nine-year-old blue merle Australian shepherd with icy-blue eyes, who had been his trusty companion and best friend for eight years, looked at him with his head tilted.

"I know it's only nine o'clock. But don't give me grief. I've spent hours on my feet in the workshop today finishing the quilt chest for Mr. O'Leary's wife's birthday."

As if he understood every word, the shepherd stood and stretched. Then he followed Maxwell from room to room as he locked the doors and turned off the lights. It had surprised Max that his father—a retired police commissioner—had worked it out where he could keep the retired K9, who the force had deemed no longer fit for service. Kicking him out the same way they had Max.

Oh, well, Maxwell had been tired of the daily grind. Even if he hadn't been called a liar and told that his career was over, he would've been looking for a change.

"Yeah, keep telling yourself that," he muttered. "You've been in these mountains for four months, and you're already bored out of your mind."

Gus barked as if agreeing with him. Max knelt and scratched the shepherd between the ears. "We just need time to get into a routine." *Come on. Who are you kidding? Four months is more than enough time to develop a routine. Admit it. You miss the hustle and bustle of the city—everything you need within walking distance. Most of all, you miss having people around.* "Starting tomorrow, we'll have a set schedule. I have a video meeting at nine with a potential client, and after that, you and I will get out and explore the area."

Only, they would stick to the hiking trails that were less traveled. He didn't need any well-meaning people to introduce themselves to him and invite him to church. Having a former partner, who'd been like a brother to him, accept bribes and frame Max for it had convinced him he wasn't as good a judge of character as he'd thought. To top it off, even his fiancée—former fiancée—had questioned his innocence. After that, Max knew he was better off without friends or a fiancée. Gus was the only companion he needed.

Standing, he led the way down the hall, the shepherd at his heels. Since leaving NYPD, it had become his custom to go to bed right after watching the late-night newscast. It was his way of trying to keep up with the events of the world. He may have left his career in law enforcement, but it didn't mean he couldn't keep up with crimes in the area, or the world, for that matter. But tonight, he felt unusually tired. He'd have to wait until morning to see what was happening in the rest of the world.

He entered his room, turned to the dog bed in the corner and pointed. "Gus, bed."

The shepherd barked, spun and raced down the hall. What was wrong with the animal? He'd never disobeyed a command before. Had Max gotten too lax with the shepherd?

Max stepped into the hall. "Gus, come!"

Ignoring the command, Gus continued on his mission. Max followed him through the living room and into the kitchen, the hairs on the nape of his neck standing at attention. What had the animal heard? Was someone outside?

Gus stopped at the back door, crouched and sniffed. Then he scratched at the door. He wasn't barking. Whatever—or whomever—was outside hadn't been deemed a threat by the animal.

Three hard knocks sounded on the door. Gus responded with a bark that was more greeting than warning.

"Help. Please, help me," a woman begged in an urgent whisper.

Was someone in real danger, or was it a hoax to get him to open the door? Maxwell bolted through the house and retrieved his Glock from his bedside table. Then he raced back to Gus's side.

"Gus, stay," he commanded.

The shepherd moved away from the door and sat at attention beside Maxwell.

"Please, hurry!" The urgency in the woman's voice intensified. "They're coming!"

He unlocked the dead bolt and opened the door. The woman barreled past him like a small tornado. It was evident she was scared of someone or something.

"Whoa. Wait! Who are you? And who is chasing you?" he demanded. He took in her appearance. Shoulder length strawberry-blond hair, frightened blue eyes, and...a baby strapped to her chest. The little girl had curly black hair, rosy cheeks and big blue eyes with tears in them. Wearing pajamas and no coat, just a pink blanket for warmth, the child watched him intently as she sucked on her thumb. However, the most disturbing thing was the rifle in the woman's hand.

"I'm Br—" She puffed out a breath. "Susan. Your neighbor. Yellow house. Through the woods. Now, please, close the door and lock it." She glanced around. "Can we turn off the hall light, too? Maybe they'll think you're not home—or asleep—and leave."

Something in her plea spurred him into action. He closed the door and bolted the lock. Then he grasped the woman—Susan—by the elbow and led her into the hall, away from any windows. "If someone is following you, there's a good chance they've already seen my lights. Turning them off now would alert them you're here."

"They want to kill me." She patted the child's back and swayed back and forth. "I barely got Rose out of the house."

"Who are *they*?"

"I don't know."

"If you don't know who they are, then why do you think they want to kill you?" he prodded.

"I heard them. The exact words were, *shut her up permanently*." A shudder racked her body.

Was she going into shock? He opened the hall closet and pulled out a blanket. Then he draped it over her shoulders. She pulled it tightly around her and the child.

He hated to press her, but he needed answers. "Why would someone want to shut you up? What do you know that they don't want revealed?"

Her brow furrowed and her eyes clouded. He could almost see the war waging inside her brain as she tried to determine how much to share with him.

"I can only help you if I know what's going on."

"Don't let the men hurt me or my child, and I'll tell you what I can."

A deep, long growl sounded behind him. He turned to see Gus looking toward the front of the house, his ears up and the hair on his back raised.

"Looks like we have company." Maxwell nodded at her weapon. "Is that thing loaded?"

"Of course it is," she declared.

"But you didn't shoot at them?"

"And risk Rose getting hit when they returned fire?"

"Fair enough." He slipped his handgun into the waistband of his jeans. "Give me your gun."

She hesitated for half a second, then held it out to him.

"Thank you. They'll expect me to be armed, but for whatever reason people tend to feel less threatened with a rifle versus a handgun." Reaching around her, he opened the door leading into the guest bathroom. "Stay here until I get back."

"Okay." She went inside and closed the door. Then he heard the lock click.

He wasn't sure what he would encounter when he went outside, but the men had surely heard Gus's barking

"Come on, Gus, let's greet our guests." He gripped the rifle by the barrel and headed to the front door. Leaving the outdoor light off, he stepped onto the porch, knowing his silhouette would be lit by the light coming from inside. Gus sat at his feet, growling. "Who's out here?"

Silence.

"I said, who's out here?" He lifted the rifle. "Don't make me ask again."

A tall man stepped out from behind a tree at the edge of the property, the full moon overhead giving off sufficient illumination to show that he had a beard but not enough to distinguish additional features. "Didn't mean to disturb you.

My wife and I got into a little tiff. She went for a walk with our little one to cool off. But I haven't seen her since. Got worried. Decided to swallow my pride and look for her. Have you seen her?"

Maxwell pressed his lips together and shook his head. The man's entire demeanor reeked of a bad con. "Don't get many visitors out this way. Haven't had the pleasure of meeting you or *your* wife. Guess I've not been very neighborly."

"It's alright."

Gus growled and walked to the edge of the porch, peering into the darkness on the side of the house.

"Your friend needs to step out of the shadows. I don't take kindly to anyone—neighbor or not—lurking around my house," Maxwell said calmly.

The tall, bearded man jerked his head, and a lanky man stepped into view.

"Want to tell me what you were doing in my backyard?"

Out of the corner of his eye, he saw the bearded man go for his weapon. Maxwell dropped the rifle, pulled his Glock from his waistband and got off a shot—hitting the tree trunk, mere inches from the man's head—before the other man could even raise his weapon. Gus barked and dove off the porch, clamping onto the lanky man's arm until he dropped his own weapon. "Get your dog off me!"

Now hiding behind the tree, the bearded man shot at Gus, thankfully missing him when the lanky man jerked his arm—Gus still attached.

"Don't shoot, Earl. You'll hit me!" the lanky man yelled to his companion.

"Gus, release!" Max commanded, diving onto the porch floor and scooting behind one of the rock pillars.

The K9 followed the command, opening his mouth and dropping to the ground. The lanky man drew back his leg as if he were going to kick the dog.

"You'll be dead before your foot connects," Max stated flatly.

The man reached for his weapon that lay at his feet where he'd dropped it. Maxwell shot the ground, inches from the man's hand. Gus bared his teeth and growled. The man cussed and disappeared into the night, leaving his gun behind.

"Gus, come." The shepherd raced to Maxwell's side. Max gave his furry friend a brief one-arm hug, thankful for the oversize pillar and the protection it provided. "Down."

The dog followed the command and lay on the porch floor beside him.

Max swung his attention back to the bearded man. "I suggest you get off my property. Whatever domestic dispute you're having needs to be settled elsewhere."

The man fired at Maxwell, hitting the rock pillar. They exchanged several rounds of gunfire before the man ran out of ammo and took off into the woods. Maxwell puffed out a breath and pushed to his feet. Stepping off the porch, he picked up the pistol the lanky man had left behind and tucked it in his waistband. Then he headed toward the front door, pausing long enough to gather the woman's rifle.

"Gus, inside!"

The shepherd followed the command, with Max on his heels. Time to confront the woman in his bathroom and find out what kind of trouble she had brought to his home.

TWO

Brenda's heart pounded in her ears as she clutched her daughter tightly. Thankfully, Rose was taking everything in stride and hadn't cried while they hid, crouched in the tub, in the home of a stranger. She'd told Rose they were playing hide-and-seek. A game the toddler always enjoyed. Even when the gunshots sounded and her eyes had rounded, Rose had quietly sucked her thumb and clung to her. Brenda had actively been trying to encourage Rose to give up her thumb sucking habit, but now was not the time to address the issue. If Rose regressed some during this time of stress, it would be okay. Brenda would start over on the process once she knew they were somewhere safe and the men after them couldn't find them.

She looked around at the modest bathroom decorated in earth tones. Barging into the home of a neighbor she'd never met was definitely something Brenda never dreamed she'd be doing tonight. It was good to know that survival skills outweighed her introvert tendencies when hers and her child's lives were in danger.

How had the men found her? She was a long way from North Carolina. And nothing in her new life connected her to the old. Except for her precious baby girl, and no one in her previous life even knew where they were or what her daughter looked like, for that matter.

Footsteps sounded in the hall. Her grip tightened around Rose. *Please, don't let that be the men who are after me.* An excited, happy sounding yelp from a dog sounded outside the bathroom door. Surely, if it were the men chasing her, the dog would growl or bark ferociously as he had earlier.

Knock. Knock. "It's safe to come out now," the homeowner said.

She stood and immediately grimaced. Her legs were numb from sitting on them in the tub.

He knocked again. "I said you're safe now."

"I know. Give me a minute, please." She stepped out of the tub, and pain shot up her leg. Biting her lip, she swallowed the cry threatening to escape.

"I'll be in the kitchen." Fading footsteps sounded in the hall.

"Mommy 'k'?" Rose patted Brenda's cheek.

"Yes, baby. Mommy is okay." She kissed the top of her daughter's head. "I love you."

"My love you." Rose puckered her lips.

Brenda leaned down and accepted the sweet baby kiss, her heart smiling at her daughter's use of *my* for *I*. Brenda was constantly surprised how quickly time passed with a child. All too soon, Rose would outgrow the babytalk stage, but for now, it was cute. "Let's go thank our neighbor for protecting us."

"T'ank him."

She hugged Rose close, thankful she was too young to realize the danger they were in. Turning toward the door, she caught a glimpse of them in the mirror over the sink. Her hair was disheveled, with two leaves sticking out of it, but it was the sight of Rose, with red cheeks and one bare foot, that almost brought Brenda to her knees.

How had she failed to notice that Rose had lost a sock somewhere along the way? Tears welled in Brenda's eyes. What was she going to do? Everything they needed to go on the run was at home, including her vehicle.

She needed to call Marshal Ackerman. He'd told her to call him if her identity had been compromised. And it most definitely had been. But she didn't even have her cell phone. And she couldn't call him in front of... She didn't know her neighbor's name. *Pull yourself together! You don't have to know his name. You just have to thank him for keeping you and Rose safe, and then you need to get as far away from here as possible.*

She settled Rose's feet on the floor, straightened and quickly pulled the leaves out of her hair. Then she splashed cold water on her face.

The sound of the dog scratching at the door drew her attention.

"Gus is worried about you. Do you think you can come out now, Susan?" the man asked softly.

Susan. After what had transpired tonight, Brenda wasn't sure she could convince her brain to think of herself as Susan Warner any longer. Not that it mattered in the long run. When Marshal Akerman relocated her, he was sure to assign her a different identity. Then she'd have to start the process of learning a new name all over again. So why bother pretending with herself? As long as she didn't slip up and reveal her true identity to anyone, what would it matter if she'd mentally become Brenda again?

She crossed to the door, unlocked it and pulled it open. "I'm sorry."

The man examined her face, concern evident in his brown eyes. She resisted the urge to squirm under his scrutiny.

"Puppy." Rose squealed and reached for the dog.

"No!" the man snapped.

Rose's bottom lip quivered, and tears sprang from her eyes.

The man shoved his hand through his hair. "I'm sorry… I didn't mean to snap. It's just, Gus isn't a pet."

Brenda reached out a hand and pulled Rose close to her side, rubbing her back. "What is he then?"

"He's a K9. Police dog. Retired, but still…"

She looked from the dog to his owner. This house had been vacant when she moved to Fisher Point and had remained vacant until four months ago. Just who was her new neighbor? If he was a police officer, could she trust him with the truth about her identity? Marshal Ackerman had told her under no circumstances was she to tell anyone the truth. The only way the US Marshals Service could guarantee her safety was if she followed their instructions. Only she *had* followed them. Every step of the way. Never deviating from the plan. So much so that she almost never thought of herself as Brenda any longer, or hadn't until tonight. She had immersed herself into being Susan Warner. And after she contacted Marshal Ackerman, she'd have to learn a new name and backstory and trick her brain into believing she was someone else for a second time.

"It's okay. We barged into your home and

you…" Her voice broke, and she met the man's gaze. "Kept the men from finding us. We'll get out of here and stop being a bother."

She tried to brush past him, but he planted his feet firmly in her path.

"What if the men are waiting on you outside? Or back at your house? What will you do then?"

"Right. Um. May I use your phone to call the police? Maybe they can pick me up and escort me back home." If she could have an officer check the inside of her home to make sure the men weren't lurking around, she could pack a few things and hit the road tonight. *And go where?*

"Look, we haven't had a proper introduction. Let's sit down and talk a few minutes. Then, if you want, we can call the police and have them meet us at your house. Okay?"

"If that's the only way you'll let me use the phone, then okay. But please, don't use that tone with my child again."

"I already apologized. I didn't mean for it to come out so sharply. K9s are—"

"Highly trained animals with a job to do. They aren't pets and shouldn't be treated as such. Like service dogs."

"Well, yeah." He raised an eyebrow. "Have you been around K9s much?"

"No. I like to watch documentaries and saw one a few months ago about service dogs."

"Can we start over? Hi, neighbor. My name is Maxwell Prescott. Max to my friends." He held out his hand and jerked his head toward the dog. "This is my trusty companion, Gus."

"Hi, Mash." Rose thrust her tiny hand into his before Susan could respond. "My is Rose."

Maxwell smiled and gently shook her daughter's hand. "Nice to meet you, Rose."

"Nice to meet you," she parroted.

He smiled and met Brenda's eyes, his dimples making her heart skip a beat. "It's nice to make your acquaintance, too, Susan. If it's okay with you, I have a small snack prepared for Rose. I thought she might enjoy that while the adults talk about what transpired here tonight. And you can explain to me who those men were and why they're after you."

Without her phone and no means of escape except through the dark woods where the men could be lying in wait, she didn't really have much choice but to go along with his suggestion. She prayed it wasn't a mistake, and that he was indeed only wanting to help.

Maxwell had left the curtains open in the living room, hoping—if they still lurked outside—the men would think he had nothing to hide and the woman and child weren't inside. But he had closed the blinds in the kitchen, knowing there would be no way to avoid walking in front of them. Leaving the lights off to cover their movements, he led the way to the small sitting nook off the kitchen where there weren't any windows.

He pointed to the small table that held a cup of milk and a saucer with a couple of chocolate chip cookies. "I didn't know if you'd want anything, but I can make coffee if you'd like."

"I'm fine. Thank you. It was thoughtful of you to prepare a snack for Rose." She went to sit on the hard wooden chair he'd pulled over from the kitchen table.

"Take the other one." Maxwell halted her, holding out a hand toward the armchair. "It will be more comfortable for the two of you. But if you want, I can go grab a blanket and make a pallet on the floor for Rose."

Susan hugged her daughter tighter. "I'll hold her."

"At least take off the harness and get comfortable."

She smiled and lifted Rose out of the contraption and sat her on the chair. "It's a toddler carrier, not a harness."

Unfastening the clips, she slipped the carrier off her arms and placed it on the floor beside the chair. Then she picked up Rose and settled into the chair with her daughter on her lap. The child stared at Maxwell with wide-eyed wonderment.

He sat on the straight-backed chair and watched as Susan offered Rose a cookie. Having dedicated the past fifteen years to his career, he hadn't spent much time around little ones, even his own nieces and nephew. Would it be appropriate to ask questions in front of her? How much of the conversation would she understand? He cleared his throat. "Um… Why don't we start by getting to know each other a little better? Like I said, my name is Maxwell Prescott. As I'm sure you're aware, I moved here four months ago."

"I had heard someone from New York City had moved in. I was kind of surprised. Moving from the bustling city to a small township in Maine must be a big change for you."

If only she knew. It wasn't the biggest change in his life. The city wasn't the only thing he'd walked away from. He'd left a career and a fiancée, both that he'd loved deeply. Until he just didn't anymore.

"It is different, but I like solitude."

"Which you had until tonight. I really am s—"

"Don't say sorry. You've already apologized. And really, there is no need. You were in danger. I'm glad Gus and I were here to help." He cocked his head. "You know where I'm from, but I don't know anything about you. If I'm not mistaken, your accent is Southern. I'm thinking maybe Tennessee or one of the Carolinas. How'd you end up in Maine?"

"I'm a single mom. I wanted to raise Rose in a small town. Fisher Point seemed perfect. Until now." She ignored his question about her accent.

What was she hiding? Why wouldn't she want anyone to know where she was from? Had she escaped an abusive relationship? Was the bearded man really her husband, as he'd implied? If so, did Susan have legal custody of Rose, or had she kidnapped her own child, keeping her from her father? He glanced at Rose.

The child munched happily on the cookie, getting crumbs and chocolate all over her face. He got up and crossed to the sink. Tearing a paper towel off the roll on the counter and wetting it, he returned to the alcove and offered it to Susan.

"Thank you." She pried the cookie from the tiny hands and wiped Rose's face. Then she handed her the cup of milk before looking back at Maxwell. "If you don't mind me using your phone, I'll call the police and report the break-in. Maybe an officer can pick us up here and escort us home."

That answered one of his questions. She wouldn't involve the police if she didn't have legal custody of her child. But it didn't mean the man earlier wasn't her ex. "What will you do if those men show back up, after your police escort leave?"

The little girl's eyes closed, and the cup in her hand tipped. Susan caught the cup and settled it back on the table before shifting her daughter so Rose's head rested on her shoulder. "We won't be there if they show back up," she mumbled.

"It's the middle of the night. Where will you go?"

"We'll be okay. I'll call Mar—my friend. He'll arrange a place for us to stay."

Just who was her friend? She'd almost said a name. Mar... Mark? Marty? No, that didn't make sense. There would be no reason for her not to say her friend's first name. It wasn't like he'd know who she was talking about if the only information she shared was a first name.

If it hadn't been a name, what had she almost said? Mar... *He'll arrange a place for us to stay.* Could it have been marshal? He narrowed his eyes. What were the chances? Only one way to find out.

He pushed to his feet, gathered the cup and the cookie plate and carried them to the sink. "I'll go grab my phone out of my bedroom. I don't keep it on me when I'm home." He turned to face her. "When you notify the marshal in charge of your protection, tell him to do a better job of hiding you and the kid next time."

Shock registered on her face. "What? How'd you know I was in witness protection?"

"I didn't. Until now." He locked gazes with her. "I'll get my phone, so you can make that call. But if it's okay with you, I'd like to speak to the marshal. And I'd also like for me and Gus to accompany you and Rose home. I'm not convinced the men are just going to slink away. And I want to be there as extra protection in case something goes wrong."

She rubbed her child's back. "Gus was a former police dog, but you weren't just his trainer, were you? You were his partner. A police officer."

The muscle in his neck twitched. He pressed his lips together and nodded. "Yeah. But that's a discussion for another time."

And hopefully, she would move to a safe house, in a different state, before they had an opportunity for that discussion. Some things were better left in the past and not discussed with people who were just passing through his life.

THREE

Her arm was numb. Rose was fast asleep—her head and upper body cradled in the crook of Brenda's left arm—and she couldn't shift her for fear of waking her. But that was the least of Brenda's worries. How could she have been so carless earlier when she'd almost said Marshal Ackerman's name? Why hadn't she covered up her blunder by hastily saying a name like Marion? Or something. It wasn't like it was her first week in WITSEC. What had been the use of the hours of writing and memorizing a detailed backstory for her and Rose, trying to trick her brain into believing she really was Susan Warner and not Brenda Granger, if she couldn't stick to the plan when things went awry?

"Did the 911 operator say how long it would take the officer to reach your house?" Maxwell's question pulled her from her self-beratement.

She glanced in his direction, spotting a deer sprinting out of the woods and freezing in the glare of the headlights. Maxwell slowed his SUV, and the animal dashed across the road.

Brenda tightened her grip on Rose. She'd always been so cautious with her child's safety and never dreamed of being placed in a position to ride in an automobile without Rose in a car seat. Thankfully—although it was farther to travel by vehicle than it had been to race in a direct path through the woods—the drive was short.

"So? What'd they say?" he prodded.

"Oh, um...ten minutes."

"It took us a bit of time to get situated and out the door. Hopefully, they won't be far behind us." He activated his blinker and slowed as he neared her driveway. "Lay your seat all the way back, so you're hidden from view."

Holding her breath, Brenda carefully shifted Rose's body so she lay against her chest. Placing her left hand flat against her daughter's tiny back, she felt along the side of the seat with her right hand until she located the electronic controls. As she pressed the button, the seat slowly reclined until she couldn't see out the windows and her upper body was lying almost completely flat.

Blue lights strobed across the dashboard.

"Looks like the police have arrived." He turned into the drive and stopped.

She detected the sound of the police vehicle

pulling in behind him. The lights now strobed on the upper half of her garage doors, which was the only part of her house she could see from her reclined position.

"Stay here," Maxwell instructed. He reached up and pressed a button near the overhead light and then exited the vehicle—the interior remaining dark.

He didn't have to tell her twice. She was perfectly happy staying out of sight with her baby in her arms. *Dear Lord, what am I going to do now? Marshal Ackerman didn't answer my call or respond to my text. He promised he'd get me out in a hurry if anything happened.* Once the officer checked out the house and deemed it safe for her to go inside, she would grab the go bag that she had hidden in the top of her closet. The backpack held a couple of changes of clothes for both her and Rose, and enough money to get them far away from here. No one had told her to have a backup plan in case something went wrong, but she'd seen enough true crime style movies to know that there wouldn't always be a hero to save the heroine.

But that didn't matter because she didn't believe in heroes anymore. She'd trusted her husband and her older brother and had always believed they were her heroes. And that had resulted in great disappointment.

Rose grunted, lifted her head, looked at Brenda with barely open eyes, then plopped her head back down on her shoulder. Brenda patted her tiny back. "It's okay, sweetie. Mommy's here. I promise to keep you safe."

Brenda lifted her upper body a few inches off the seat, straining her neck to peek outside. Maxwell stood at the back of the vehicle talking to two officers in hushed tones.

"I should have called sooner," Maxwell said, loud enough for her to hear. "One of the men said he was looking for his wife and child. But my neighbor insists she doesn't know the man. And the entire situation seemed…fishy."

"You did the right thing," the officer replied, in a volume that matched Maxwell's. "Wait in your vehicle, and we'll check the house. Once we finish, we'll interview the woman."

The door opened, and Maxwell slid into the seat. "I know you're uncomfortable, but you need to stay low a little longer," he whispered. "Your front door was open, so the officers are going to check inside."

She nodded but didn't look in his direction as she continued to watch the pattern of the eerie blue lights flashing on her garage door. Brenda hoped the officers would clear the house quickly and allow her inside. Rose's nighttime diaper felt wet and would need to be changed soon.

Sometime later, there was a rap on the passenger side window. Brenda startled, and Rose let out a whimper. Maxwell lowered the window, and an officer squatted and peered inside.

"Sorry, ma'am." The officer braced his arms on the door.

"It's okay." She pressed the button on the side of the seat until it had returned to its upright position. "Is it safe to go inside now?"

"There are no signs of the intruders, but they ransacked your house. If you're ready to go inside, we'll go through the house with you and see if anything is missing. Then we'll get your statement and any information you may have about the men responsible."

"Okay." She unfastened her seat belt and turned to Maxwell. "Thank you for everything."

The vein in his neck twitched. He met her gaze, and her heart slammed against her rib cage as she really examined his chiseled features for the first time. His brown eyes darkened as if a storm were brewing. Had she said something wrong?

"I think it's best if I stick around until your *friend* arrives to pick you and Rose up." Maxwell jumped out of the SUV and jogged around the vehicle.

The officer stood, opened her door and stepped aside, looking from her to Maxwell and back again.

"Thank you." She supported Rose's back and hurriedly made her way along the path to the front door.

Walking into her home, Brenda gasped. Everything had happened so quickly earlier that she hadn't taken in the destruction in the living areas of her home. Books and knickknacks had been pulled off the built-in shelves lining either side of the fireplace and strewn about the room. The armchair had been turned upside down. Sofa cushions had been sliced with a knife and the foam stuffing tossed to the floor. What could the men have been searching for? One had mentioned a microchip, but she had no clue what he was talking about. Obviously, there was much more to the break-in than the men's desire to kill her.

When she'd first been approached about going into witness protection, she'd thought the officers involved in the case against her husband and her brother were being overly cautious. It had actually taken them a couple of days to convince her it was in her newborn daughter's best interest for them to disappear. And to be honest, she hadn't agreed because she feared for her and Rose's lives. What had enticed her to go along with the plan they had laid out before her had been the knowledge that she could walk down the street or into church without people pointing at her and her child whispering about them being related to murderers.

The state of her house emphasized the authorities had been correct about the danger, and she'd simply been living in denial. The people running the drug ring were hunting for something they thought she had. They wouldn't stop until they found it. And—in the words of Earl—*shut her up, permanently.*

Her knees buckled. Strong hands grasped her upper arms and guided her to the wooden rocking chair near the fireplace—the fire had died out and only embers remained. Dropping onto the chair, she glanced up, looking into the same brown eyes she'd locked gazes with moments earlier. Only the storm clouds she'd seen inside them when she'd barged into his house had been replaced with pity. The one thing she hated most in this world was other people's pity.

Thirty minutes later, Maxwell and Gus paced the width of the living room, waiting. The officers had left after taking their statements and receiving the weapon that had been left behind by the lanky man. Maxwell hoped they would be able to identify the man from fingerprints or the serial number on the weapon, but he knew there was no guarantee of that happening.

What was taking Susan so long to pack a few

things for her and the little one? And where was her handler? She'd left him a cryptic message when she'd been unable to reach him. Had he called her back? Maybe Max should go check on her? Packing was taking much too long.

He headed down the hall toward the bedrooms. The door to the little girl's room was open and light spilled out. He peered inside.

Susan stuffed diapers into an oversize bag. "We better take as many supplies as we can, Rose. There's no telling where we'll end up or what will be available when we get there." She paused, leaned over the railing of the baby bed and ruffled her daughter's hair.

"Mommy." Rose held up her arms.

Susan captured one of the tiny hands and kissed it. "Just one more minute. I need to pack a few toys. Okay?"

"Hoppy." The little girl picked up a stuffed kangaroo and hugged it tightly.

Susan turned and gasped, catching sight of him in the doorway.

"I'm sorry. Didn't mean to startle you. I was wondering what was taking so long. Can I help?"

"No." She shook her head and zipped up the bag. Then she placed it on the floor beside a backpack that rested against the dresser. "I just need to grab a few more things for Rose and then I'm ready. Thank you for sticking around long enough for me to pack and get on the road."

She pulled a small pink princess rolling suitcase out of the closet, crossed to a glider in the corner, placed the suitcase on the ottoman and unzipped it.

"Do you know where you're headed?" He wasn't sure why he asked, because he knew she couldn't share the information with anyone. Not if she wanted to keep herself and her daughter safe.

"No. Far from here." Opening drawers, she worked quickly to fill the suitcase with Rose's clothes and a few stuffed animals and books. "I'll drive through the night and find a safe place to stop tomorrow."

"Wait." He crossed to her and placed a hand on her arm. "Didn't you call the marshal again?"

Susan pulled free of his touch and turned back to her task. "I did. From my phone, after the officers left. But he didn't answer. He may be busy with another case or something."

Rose, who'd pulled herself up to stand in the crib, watched the adults intently. He really hated to have another serious discussion in front of the child. Even though he doubted she'd understand the conversation, he knew she'd pick up on the tone. His parents had never once argued in front of him or his sister. Although he remembered hearing them having heated discussions behind their closed bedroom door, and it had always upset him. But this discussion couldn't wait. And in reality, he was only passing through the little girl's life for a moment in time. Hopefully, she would not have any lingering memories of the night.

"You can't just vanish without talking to him." Max shoved his hand through his hair, still getting used to it being longer than how he'd always worn it while working for the PD. "There are rules about being in the program."

"Yeah. What do you know about it?" She glared at him. "You know nothing about what I've been through. I can't sit here and wait to hear from him. What if the men come back?"

"You and Rose can come back to my house until your handler returns your call."

"Do you really think the men won't return and watch your house? If I don't get in my car and drive as far away as possible, something bad will happen. To us, and to you. I can't have that on my conscience." She shoved a drawer closed. "Rose and I have to disappear. Tonight."

Rose's little bottom lip puckered and quivered, then she burst into tears. Susan picked her up and rubbed her back, whispering incoherent words of comfort into her ear. Then she turned to glare at him as if it were his fault the child was upset. He puffed out a breath.

"I don't want to argue, but just like you don't want to be responsible for anything happening to me, I can't sit back and let you and your daughter drive off into the night. I may not be employed as a police officer at the moment, but I took an oath to protect." She opened her mouth, and he rushed on before she could protest. "I'll go with you. Wherever you want to go. Then, if you haven't heard from Marshal...?"

"Ackerman. But I don't—"

"I'll load your luggage." Maxwell picked up the bag and the backpack before she could argue. He'd noticed the compact SUV in the garage earlier. And though he didn't want to say anything to her, he wanted to check it out and make sure the men hadn't tampered with it. "Where are your keys?"

Susan reached into the front pocket of her jeans, extracted her key ring and held it out to him. Good, she wasn't going to fight him.

"Hurry. Okay?"

She nodded.

Without giving her a chance to complain, he charged out of the room. "Stay," he ordered Gus as he sprinted down the hall. Without looking back, he knew the K9 would follow his command and protect the woman and child.

Maxwell completed as thorough of a check of the vehicle as the cramped garage space allowed—looking underneath for explosives and oil or fluid stains on the concrete then checking under the hood for signs of tampering. The doorknob on the door leading into the garage rattled, and he slammed the hood closed seconds before Susan stepped into the small, confined space. Rose toddled beside her with Gus trailing behind.

"Did you finish?"

"Finish what?"

She smiled, tossed the small suitcase into the cargo space and closed the hatch he'd left open when he'd placed the other two bags inside earlier. "Did you finish inspecting my vehicle to see if they tampered with it?"

"You're very observant. And smart. Backing your vehicle into the garage so you could pull straight out when you left was a good idea."

"I had groceries. It's easier to unload them, if I back in." She moved to the passenger side of the vehicle and opened the back door.

"Go bye-bye," Rose squealed as she climbed into the SUV, settling into her car seat so her mother could fasten her in.

After she finished, Susan stepped back and put her hand on the doorframe.

"Wait," he commanded. "Gus, in."

The Australian shepherd hopped inside the vehicle and settled into the back seat beside the child. Rose laughed. "Puppy!"

Gus was long past the puppy stage, but there was no point telling the little girl that.

"Okay, let's go." He turned to go around the vehicle, but Susan grabbed his arm.

"I'm driving."

"It's best if I drive. We don't know what situation we'll encounter. The men could follow us."

"First, it's my vehicle, with my child inside. Second, I am a very experienced driver. I have good reflexes. Grew up on a farm, dodging cows and horses while learning to drive in the pasture."

"But these are curvy mountain roads—"

"No more so than the ones I drove on before moving here." She held out her hand, palm upward. "Third, if we run into trouble and you need to use your weapon, it will be easier if you're not the one behind the wheel."

Arguing with her would be a waste of time. He dropped the key into her outstretched hand. She moved around the back of the SUV to the driver's side door.

A loud bang sounded inside the house. Their eyes met over the roof of the vehicle. He slipped his gun from the shoulder holster he'd put on under his jacket before they left his house.

Should he investigate the sound and confront the men or stick with the woman and child? Susan had already hit the garage door opener and pressed the start button on the SUV. He jumped inside, immediately lowering his window, ready to shoot if necessary.

Once the garage door was just high enough the vehicle could scoot under it, Susan floored the gas. They raced out of the garage as the bearded man appeared in the doorway leading into the kitchen. The man shot at them, the bullet going through the rear window and hitting the back seat headrest.

"Go, go, go!" Maxwell yelled, sticking his upper body out the open window and firing off multiple shots in rapid succession.

Bearded Guy turned to dive behind the kitchen door and collided with the lanky guy who had appeared behind him. Both men fell to the floor as the garage door closed.

Maxwell turned around and settled into his seat. "Smart thinking, closing the garage door."

Pulling out of the driveway, she turned right. "I thought it might be harder for him to hit us if he couldn't see us."

Maxwell looked back just in time to see the two men racing out of the house. "You better floor it. They won't be far behind."

Dear Lord, what have I gotten mixed up in?

When he'd left law enforcement, he'd promised himself he'd never get drawn back in again. But he couldn't abandon a woman and child in need. He'd find a place for them to hide out for the night. Tomorrow, if Susan still hadn't reached the marshal assigned to her, Maxwell would deliver her and Rose to the nearest US Marshals Office. Then he would arrange a ride back home for him and Gus, and they would go back to their hermit existence.

FOUR

Maxwell watched as Susan glanced in the rearview mirror, her face losing all color. Twisting in his seat, he spotted the bullet hole in the back window, slightly higher than the top of the little girl's car seat. If the bullet had been inches lower, it would have hit her. He turned back to Susan. She had a death grip on the steering wheel. "Breathe."

"What?" She looked at him questioningly.

The vehicle veered right. She turned her attention to the road and gently guided the SUV back into the lane. Impressive. Most people, unless properly trained, would have jerked the wheel and risked losing control on the ice and snow.

"I didn't mean to distract you. I only wanted to encourage you to take a few slow, focused breaths…you know, to settle your nerves." Max scratched his head.

He sounded ridiculous. Why was he tossing out the same hokey advice his mom had bombarded him with when they suspended him from the force? When a person was in a stressful situation, the last thing they needed was someone telling them how to deal with their emotions.

"Thank you," she whispered. "You're right. I was allowing fear to take over when I should have been thanking God. The bullet *didn't* hit Rose. My child is alive. And we need to keep her that way."

Should have been thanking God. He pressed his lips together. *Keep your thoughts to yourself. Let her believe God is protecting her and her child if it gives her peace.*

The little girl was chattering away in the back seat. Maxwell had no clue what she was saying, but he noted Gus had climbed onto the seat beside her and placed his head on her lap. The animal had always displayed a need to comfort people in times of trauma. He was thankful that Gus was keeping the little one occupied. While Max didn't know much about children and what events in early childhood would be stored in their little brains as lifetime memories, he suspected, if a memory from this early in life could become permanent, something as impactful as being shot at and chased by evil men would be that memory. Unless the interaction with Gus could override it. Or unless they could avoid future run-ins with the men after Susan.

"They won't be far behind us. If we don't get off the main road, they'll catch us." Max stated the obvious.

"I'll do my best to lose them. Unfortunately, the only roads intersecting this one for the next ten miles only lead to houses and don't really go anywhere."

"What?" He glanced around. "Why would you go this way?"

"Because it's the only way out of town at the moment. Don't you think I'd take a more direct route if there was one? Or do you think I enjoy putting my daughter's life in danger?" She glared at him briefly before turning her eyes back to the road. The predicted snow had started falling while she'd packed, and there was already an inch of fresh powder on the roadways, covering the icy spots left behind after the last winter weather event.

Getting into a fight with her wouldn't accomplish anything other than amping up her already jagged nerves. Besides, even though he'd lived in the small township for four months, he hadn't ventured out much. And he definitely didn't know the area that well. "I'm sorry. I—"

"I shouldn't have—" she said simultaneously.

Susan blew out a breath. "I'm sorry. I shouldn't have been snippety. I...they could have hit Rose..."

Her voice cracked, and she brushed her cheeks with the back of one hand.

He did not want to see her cry. A woman crying was like kryptonite to him. Not that he thought he was Superman or anything, but the sight of a woman in tears always brought him to his knees.

Maxwell settled squarely into the seat, clicked his seat belt into place and rolled up his window, cutting off the bitter, icy wind that had been blowing through the interior of the small SUV. "It's okay. I shouldn't have questioned you. But...why is this the only way out of town *at the moment*?"

"You don't know?" she asked incredulously.

Frowning, he shook his head. What had he missed? "No."

"I guess you really are a hermit." The snow shower intensified, and she activated the windshield wipers. "There was a mudslide, the other side of town, three days ago. It blocked both lanes of the road. There's a detour around it, but it's curvy back roads I'd rather avoid in the dark."

"That makes sense." The snow was falling harder, and her grip tightened on the steering wheel. "You're doing great. Just keep your eyes on the road ahead of us. I'll keep my eyes on the road behind us."

She nodded.

Silence blanketed the inside of the vehicle and soon he heard soft baby snores coming from the back seat. He glanced over his shoulder. Gus's head still rested on the child's lap. His eyes were closed, but Max knew he was in tune with the child and would alert the instant he felt the little girl was in danger.

As Max turned back around, he caught sight of lights in the distance. "We have company," he announced calmly, almost as if he were discussing the weather.

A dark colored SUV sped toward them, disregarding the icy road conditions that had kept their speed just under the maximum limit. It could only be the men after them. It's unlikely anyone else would drive as recklessly on these roads at this time of night.

"What do I do?" Susan asked urgently.

"Focus on driving. Let me worry about the men." He unfastened his seat belt.

"What are you doing?" she demanded. "It's too dangerous for you to be unbuckled. There could be patches of ice on the road."

Grabbing hold of the back of his seat, he twisted sideways to fit through the small opening between the front seats. "Just keep us out of the ditch." He grunted. "Gus, move."

The shepherd pressed closer to the now wide-awake child, making room for Max in the back seat.

"Puppy!" Rose squealed, and buried her tiny hands into the fur on Gus's back.

"His name is Gus. Can you call him Gus?" With one final push, he made it into the back seat, and instantly rubbed Gus's hindquarters. He would have to give him a treat after this was all over. "Good boy."

"Gus. Puppy name. Gus." Rose rubbed vigorously on the shepherd's head.

When the situation wasn't as dire, Maxwell would have to teach the child how to be gentle with the canine. But he knew, even if she was rough, Gus would not nip at her. As was a common characteristic of his breed, he had always demonstrated a protective nature, especially around children.

Maxwell twisted in his seat so he could have a clear view of the vehicle behind them. "You really don't have a clue who these guys are? Their names or anything?"

"Only their first names. I overheard them talking. The bearded guy is Earl, and the other one is Jed."

While not a major clue, having their first names was beneficial. Now he'd be able to keep their antics straight without thinking of them as Bearded Guy and Slender Guy.

"There's a road up ahead that goes around the lake," Susan announced. "It's a gravel road. Narrow in spots. But there are several smaller roads that branch off it, leading to cabins. Do you want me to take it? Or stay on the main road?"

The vehicle behind them was gaining fast. He did not want to be trapped on a side road where he didn't know all the exit routes. "Is there a police station or a hospital nearby?"

"The police station is about twenty miles away. And the hospital is farther than that."

She tightened her grip on the wheel. The adrenaline rushing through her had to be double what was coursing through his veins. He was a trained police officer. She was not. And while he didn't want anything to happen to either her or Rose, he had just met them so his emotions weren't involved. She was a mom with a child to protect, one who needed her to remain alive.

"I need a decision soon. The turn is coming up." She met his eyes in the rearview mirror. "The men are gaining fast. I don't want them close enough to shoot at us again."

"Take the gravel road," he ordered. "Don't give a blinker, and if you can do so safely, don't touch your brakes until the last second. We don't want them to know what we're doing until it's too late for them to follow us."

"You've got it."

The road came into view. Susan kept her speed even and steady and, as he had instructed, turned the wheel at the last second, the front tires skidding as they met the loose gravel. He watched as she calmly regained control of the wheel. Someone had taught her how to drive in a variety of situations. He was sure there was a story to be told. Maybe he'd get her to tell him later. If there was time before the Marshals Service transferred her to a new location.

The tires gained traction, and she drove along the rutted gravel road. He glanced out the rear window and watched as the other SUV passed them. The driver slammed on his brakes and the vehicle skidded on the icy road, spinning around and around like an ice skater performing a triple axel before landing in the ditch on the opposite side of the road. The grille of the vehicle crushed against a giant pine tree.

Relief briefly washed over him. He didn't know how she'd managed such a maneuver, but Susan had temporarily bought them time to escape. He was sure the men would come after them with a renewed vengeance once they were back on the road. Although, he suspected they would have to get a replacement vehicle.

Maybe he'd pry Susan for more information about her past than simply her driving skills. She said she didn't know who was after her. If he could figure it out, he'd stand a better chance of stopping them for good.

Brenda's heart pounded like a bongo drum in her chest. She released a breath, silently counting to eight as she did so. The road was narrow and bumpy, but the tires seemed to have better traction on the gravel road than they'd had on the paved one. Now, she just needed to remember the correct road to take that would lead her out of the maze of driveways and back onto the highway on the other end of the lake.

Rose giggled in the back seat. Looking into the mirror, she saw the dog lick her daughter's face in a gentle kiss. Brenda had thought about getting a dog for protection but had been hesitant because she'd been afraid that a guard dog might be too dangerous to have around a small child. Could she have been wrong? Maybe she'd ask Max for suggestions on low-maintenance protective breeds.

"Watch out. I'm climbing back into the front." Maxwell came between the seats, feetfirst, and plopped into the one he'd vacated earlier. Then he clicked his seat belt into place and turned toward her. "Whew. That was pretty amazing. You weren't lying when you said you could drive. I couldn't have done any better myself."

"Thank you." She chuckled. "If my brother could see me now, he'd be surprised. And, maybe, a little proud."

"Where is your brother?" he asked conversationally.

"In pris—" She inhaled sharply. The events of the evening had ripped a hole in the invisible veil she'd wrapped tightly around her past, unraveling it to where she'd almost shared personal background information with someone she had only known for a couple of hours. "I…uh… I'd rather not talk about it."

Focusing on the road ahead, her cheeks warmed under his gaze. She appreciated his help more than she could ever express. Hiding her and Rose and, now, traveling with them to make sure they stayed safe until she could contact Marshal Ackerman was above and beyond being neighborly. But she'd already given away too much by even letting him guess that she and Rose were in WITSEC. If he let on to Marshal Ackerman that he knew anything about her past, the marshal might kick her out of the program.

Rounding a bend in the road, her headlights lit upon a large pine tree that had fallen across the road. She slammed on the brakes, the back tires fishtailing before the vehicle came to a stop, inches from the tree that blocked their path.

"Whew." She breathed heavily, put the vehicle into Park and turned to check on Rose. "Are you okay, sweetie?"

"My 'k', Mommy."

Brenda smiled. She'd been trying to teach Rose to say *I* instead of *my* when referencing herself, but right this instant there were no sweeter words than *my 'k', Mommy*.

The passenger side door opened, and Maxwell exited the vehicle. Watching as he examined every angle of the tree and tugged on a few limbs, she knew he was trying to figure out their options. There was no need for her to get out in the cold and look, too. Whatever he decided was their best course of action was fine with her, as long as they got moving soon. Brenda peered into the dark shadows of the woods bordering the road. Could they go off-road and go around the tree? She'd purposefully bought a four-wheel drive vehicle, so she'd have less risk of being stranded in the winter months when it snowed. She wasn't sure about driving in the muddy woods, but if that's what had to be done, then so be it.

A few minutes later, Maxwell climbed back into the SUV. "I don't see a way around the tree."

"I have a chain in the back. Maybe we can pull it off the road."

"I doubt it. It's massive." He met her gaze. "I don't think a vehicle this size could do the job."

"But we have to try," she insisted.

"And risk damaging your vehicle?"

"So, I lose a bumper. That's better than having to turn around and running into those men again."

"Losing a bumper is the best-case scenario. Worst case, you mess up your transmission and we're stranded here." He released a breath. "Look, I'm not eager to face those guys again either, but their vehicle was damaged pretty badly when they landed in the ditch. I doubt it's drivable. They've probably called a tow truck. Hopefully, they'll be gone before we reach them."

"If they're not?" She held her breath, afraid of the answer. *I will never forgive you, Joe, for turning me into someone who lets fear rule their life.*

"I won't let them get to you. Or Rose. Trust me."

He clasped her hand between both of his, and even though his hands were cold from being outside, a warm sense of security settled over her. In that instant, she trusted him. Although she wasn't sure why. How could she trust a man she didn't know? Her husband and her brother—

men she'd known her entire life—who had an obligation to protect her, had both failed her and her daughter. Brenda would never let any man have sole control over her protection, ever again.

"Okay, I'll turn around and head back to the main road. *But* here's the plan." She pulled her hand free from his. "Less than a quarter mile from the main road, there is a side road that leads to a picnic area. I'll pull in there. You can hike through the woods to the road and check things out."

He looked thoughtful for a moment. "Okay. But I'm leaving Gus with you. And you have to keep your rifle within reach."

She gasped. "I left my rifle in your vehicle."

Maxwell shook his head. "I transferred it to yours while you were packing. It looked old. I thought it might be something you'd want to keep, but also, I thought you might need it for protection."

"Thank you. It's Grandpa Henry's rifle. I'd hate to lose it." Brenda shifted into reverse and backed away from the tree.

"I'm surprised you were allowed to keep it. I thought WITSEC had a strict *no guns* policy."

Backing up a few feet, she turned the wheel and inched forward and then repeated the process—backing up, turning, moving forward, backing again—until she'd completed a multipoint turn to get her small SUV turned around. Once she was headed the opposite direction, she spared him a quick glance. "I didn't ask permission."

No point trying to hide the truth, but she wouldn't reveal who Grandpa Henry was. Let Max think the rifle was a family heirloom or something. She didn't want anyone to be upset with Henry Bauer—a sweet elderly man from church who, along with his wife, Memaw Linda, had become honorary grandparents to her and Rose. When Henry had learned that she was a widow—her WITSEC cover story long before Joe was murdered—and lived alone with Rose in a house in the woods, he'd insisted on letting her borrow the rifle for protection from wild animals and intruders. After the events of the evening, she'd be forever grateful to him. She prayed she could thank him one day.

"When you're in witness protection, you're not allowed to bring a suitcase or anything. How would you slip something as large as a rifle past the marshal assigned to your case?"

The road to the picnic area came into view. She turned onto it, and her vehicle bounced over the uneven, rutted path. Reaching the end of the short road, she circled the parking area so her SUV pointed toward the exit. Then she put the vehicle into Park, but left the engine running.

Brenda turned to face him. "How I slipped a rifle past my handler isn't important at the moment. Can we, please, focus on the matter at hand? Like getting past the men with guns without getting shot at again?"

He stared at her, and a muscle in his jaw twitched. Then he nodded. "Turn off the overhead light so it doesn't come on when I open the door."

She did as Maxwell instructed. He got out, leaving his door open, walked to the back of the vehicle and retrieved the rifle. Returning, he leaned in and placed the rifle on the passenger seat. Then he looked at Gus. "Guard."

Instantly, the dog sat at attention on the back seat.

"Gus will protect you. If you hear someone in the woods, open the door and give the command *seek*." Maxwell held his hand out to her. "May I have your phone?"

Why would he ask for her phone? She pulled it out of her back pocket and placed it on his palm, watching intently. Opening the text app, he sent a message and then handed it back to her. His phone dinged. He pulled it out of his pocket and pressed down on the button on the side to silence it. "Now you have my number. If something happens and you have to take off, I'll be able to call you."

"What about Gus? Do I leave him if he's out chasing someone in the woods?"

"Give the command *come*, and he'll return to the vehicle. Keep him with you."

"Okay." She nodded, every nerve in her body on high alert.

Maxwell tipped his head, straightened, softly closed the door and disappeared into the night. An uneasy feeling of vulnerability settled over her as she realized, for the second time tonight, she was alone in the woods with her child. Well, and another person's dog.

"'The Lord is my shepherd; I shall not want,'" she whispered, reciting the twenty-third Psalm—something she'd started doing after she'd entered WITSEC to ease her anxiety and remind herself God was in control. "'He maketh me to lie down in green pastures…'"

FIVE

Maxwell worked his way through the woods, headed toward the main road they had turned off earlier, thankful there was several inches of snow to cushion his steps. As he neared the road, he saw flashing yellow lights. A wrecker. Where were the Earl and Jed? He made his way to a large Colorado blue spruce and hid behind it, peeking around to assess the scene before him. The wrecker had parked across both lanes of the two-lane highway, and the driver was busy hooking the pulley system to the back bumper of the SUV.

He spotted the silhouettes of Earl and Jed standing at the edge of the ditch. They seemed to be in a heated discussion as they watched the driver work. The wrecker was between them and the gravel road, which could be a factor in his and Susan's favor. If she would let him get behind the wheel, he was confident he could drive out of their current hiding place and get past the men before either one of them could react. Turning, he charged through the woods, ignoring the cold, wet snow soaking his pant legs and shoes. His lungs burned from breathing in the cold air, but he needed to reach the woman and her child quickly.

As he burst into the clearing, Gus raced up to him. Susan must have heard him coming and feared he was one of the men with guns. She had done exactly as he had directed and let the K9 out to protect her. Reaching down, he scratched Gus between his ears. "Good boy."

He lifted his hand and waved, so Susan would know it was him. Then he walked up to the SUV, opened the back door and commanded Gus to get inside. Closing the door, he rapped his knuckles on the driver's side door.

She lowered the window. "Did—"

"Would—"

They spoke in unison.

He bent slightly at the waist so he could see her clearly. "I'll answer all of your questions, but we need to get out of here, fast."

"Then why are you standing around? Get in," she ordered.

"Would you let me drive? Please."

After a couple of long seconds, she nodded, released her seat belt and exited the vehicle.

Then, without a word, she jogged around the front of the SUV and slid into the passenger seat.

"Thank you." He settled behind the steering wheel and quickly adjusted the seat, rearview mirror and side mirrors to accommodate his longer frame.

Pulling out of the picnic area, he took a left toward the main road. "A wrecker is blocking the road, and the men are focused on watching the driver work. Since your vehicle is a hybrid and is quiet, they won't have much warning about our approach. Hopefully, they won't know we're coming their way until they see the headlights. Which means they'll see us leave but won't be able to do anything about it."

"What will stop them from shooting at us again? I can't risk Rose getting hit."

"It's a bigger risk to Rose if we simply sit around and wait for them to find us. They may be temporarily immobile, but I guarantee you they will remedy the situation and be after you again."

He slowed the vehicle as he neared the stop sign but did not come to a complete stop. With a quick glance toward the wrecked vehicle, he turned right and raced away from the wreckage. In the rearview mirror, he saw the two men run to the front of the wrecker. The headlights illuminated Jed as he raised his gun, but Earl grabbed his hand and stopped him, probably because of the presence of the tow truck driver.

"You did it!" Susan yelled excitedly.

"Did it," Rose echoed.

Susan loosened her seat belt and reached into the back seat.

"What are you doing?" He tightened his hands on the wheel. Maxwell would prefer her to sit in her seat and stop moving around like that, especially while he drove on slick roads.

"I was handing Rose her kangaroo toy and tucking the blanket around her." She turned in her seat and faced forward, tightening the seat belt once more. "I'm hoping she will go to s-l-e-e-p."

S-l-e-e-p, he repeated in his head, stringing the letters together. Sleep. A smile crept on his face as he recalled his sister spelling words around her children. Maxwell imagined Rose would drift off soon, as it was nearing eleven o'clock.

"Where do we go now? You do realize we're headed toward the mudslide area, right?"

"We'll figure out a way around it." He pulled his cell phone out of his pocket, quickly glanced at the screen, so it would unlock the device, and handed it to her. Desperate times called for desperate measures. "Open the text message app, scroll to the text thread labeled Dad."

She did as he'd instructed. "Okay, now what?"

Silently releasing a breath, he pushed away his fears that she would read the messages between him and his father, where Dad kept asking him to come home. No one needed to know what a poor excuse for a son he'd become, turning his back on everyone and everything. "If you click on the top, on the picture icon of my father, it will open a details page. Scroll down until you see the *Photos* heading and—"

"You realize that I actually know how cell phones work, right? You could've just told me to look for a photo." She blew out a breath. "I'm sorry. That sounded rude. What is the photo I'm searching for?"

"It's okay. I should've asked and not assumed. You're looking for a photo that's a screenshot of an address in Waterford."

She scrolled through the photos. "Found it."

"Open the maps app and enter the address."

"If it's okay with you, I'll put it on my phone since it's synced with the vehicle. That way, you'll be able to see the directions as well as hear them."

"That would be good. Thanks."

Soon, the directions were on the screen, and the tension in his shoulders lessened. As long as his cousin Tim didn't have an off-season tenant at his rental cabin, they should be able to stay there for a few days.

"So what is this place where we're going?"

"It's a vacation rental cabin. Belongs to a relative. I spent a couple of weeks there last year while I was trying to decide if I wanted to move to Maine. Since this is the offseason, it should be vacant so we can stay there until you reach the marshal in charge of protecting you."

"Shouldn't you call your relative to ask permission to use the cabin?"

Max spared a quick glance in her direction. "If it weren't the middle of the night, I would. Look, I'm positive he would say it was okay for us to use his place. He and his wife have a new baby—a three-month-old boy—which is another reason I won't call him this late. But I know he wouldn't want Rose, or you, out in the cold tonight."

She seemed satisfied with his answer, and a blanket of silence settled over the vehicle. A little while later, the soft puffing sound of Gus's snore disrupted the quiet.

Susan twisted in her seat. "Looks like your dog and my daughter are both asleep."

"I'm not surprised." A smile lifted one corner of his mouth as he recalled the Australian shepherd sleeping on a pile of gravel in a rail yard on a frosty December night when they were undercover, trying to bust a ring of human traffickers. "Gus can sleep anywhere. But no worries, he's a light sleeper and will wake up at the slightest hint of trouble. Usually, before I'm even aware danger is approaching. It's what makes him a great K9." Maxwell frowned.

"Made," he muttered under his breath. Gus had been a top-notch police dog. Now he was a retired has-been just like Max.

"Did you say something?" Susan queried.

"Nothing important." He glanced at the map on the display screen. "Looks like we should reach my cousin's cabin shortly after midnight. Hopefully, after a good night's rest, we'll be able to come up with a clear plan for your safety."

Then he and Gus could go back to their quiet life in the woods, unencumbered by what was going on in the rest of the world.

Brenda sat in her vehicle, the engine and heat still running as she watched Maxwell knock on the door of the cabin. "Hurry," she muttered under her breath, wrapping her arms tightly around her middle.

She understood his need to be certain no one was occupying the rental. However, there were no lights on and there wasn't a vehicle in sight. Surely that meant the cabin was vacant.

Even though she doubted the men chasing her

could find them here since they couldn't trace the cabin to her, she felt vulnerable sitting in the SUV.

Brenda took in her surroundings. There was a larger cabin to the left and woods to the right. There were no cars at the other cabin either, so she suspected it was also a vacation rental. Did it belong to Maxwell's cousin as well?

Her door opened, and she jumped. Lost in thought, she hadn't seen Maxwell approach.

"Come on, let's get inside." He opened the back passenger door.

The Australian shepherd hopped out and trotted to the edge of the woods to do his business.

"I'll grab the bags from the back while you carry Rose inside."

"I only need the backpack." She bent inside the vehicle and unfastened a still-sleeping Rose.

Pulling her child close and wrapping her arms tightly around her, Brenda hurried toward the small cabin. Maxwell had left the door open, and she stepped into a small vestibule that was dimly lit.

"Go on inside," he instructed as he approached.

"The rest of the house is dark. Without knowing my way around, I'm afraid to venture farther. Don't want to bump into things." Heat crept up her neck. She did not want him to think she was afraid of the dark, but she could not risk falling with Rose.

"Sorry. I should've turned on more lights. I was in a hurry to let you in." He reached around her and opened the door that led from the vestibule into the cabin. "The light switch is just inside the door on your right."

Shifting Rose, she freed her hand, reached out and felt for the switch. Locating it, she clicked it on. Light flooded the room, and Brenda moved farther inside to allow Max to enter.

He propped her rifle in the corner near the door and placed the bag on the coffee table. Then he disappeared back into the vestibule, and she heard the dead bolt click into place. Returning to the living room, he closed and locked the interior door as well. "If you can give me a few minutes to make sure all the doors and windows are locked, I'll show you to the bedroom."

Tightening her grip on Rose, Brenda nodded.

He went about his task, returning a few minutes later. "This is a one-bedroom, one-bathroom cabin. There's a Murphy bed in the loft, but I think it's best if we stay together."

"Rose and I can take the Murphy bed." She was not about to share her room with a man.

He scrubbed a hand over his face. "I didn't mean that I would share a room with you. You and Rose will take the bedroom. I'll be fine on the couch. I don't expect the men to find us here, but if they do, I want to be able to get to you quickly. We might stand a better chance of escaping if we're both on the first floor somewhat close to each other."

"Of course. I wasn't thinking." Embarrassment washed over her. Even though she had only known him for a few hours, he had done nothing to make her feel threatened or endangered since their meeting. She should have known his intentions were honorable. Brenda glanced down at her daughter, who'd fallen asleep on her shoulder. "I guess I should put Rose to bed."

"The bedroom is just down the hall, second door on the right. The restroom is the first door."

Slipping the backpack strap over her shoulder, she turned and headed down the hall, Gus following at her feet. Stopping, she looked down at the shepherd. "Where are you going?"

He sat and looked up at her, his head tilted and his blue eyes assessing her.

"Looks like he's decided it's his job to guard Rose," Maxwell walked up behind her.

She looked from the dog to his owner and back again. Brenda had never had a dog before. Her brother had been allergic so their parents had rejected the idea any time she'd brought it up. And an Alaskan husky had bitten Joe when he was a small child, so he'd also vehemently rejected the idea of having a dog after they had married. When she became a single parent, she hadn't had the energy to add a dog to her household.

"I can make him stay with me." Maxwell grabbed hold of Gus's collar. "But he'll probably end up sleeping in the hall outside the bedroom door. So don't trip over him if you have to go to the restroom in the middle of the night."

"It's already the middle of the night." She smiled and shook her head. "I guess, since he only wants to protect Rose, it will be okay for him to sleep in the room with us."

Realizing she had no clue what the dog's sleeping habits were, Brenda met Maxwell's eyes. "He won't expect to sleep in the bed with us, will he?"

A smile split his face. "No. He'll be fine on the floor beside the bed. If there's an extra pillow, you might offer it to him, but if not, he'll be fine."

"Good night, then."

"Good night."

She went into the bedroom and closed the door behind Gus, leaving Maxwell standing in the hall. A few minutes later, she heard his footsteps retreating. Then she crossed to the bed and placed Rose on top of the covers on the side farthest from the door.

Gus trotted around the bed and laid on the floor nearest Rose. What a strange turn of events this night had taken. Earlier in the evening, she'd been full of self-pity over the loss of the life she'd dreamed of having with the man she'd loved. Anger over the situation he'd put her in would probably never completely dissipate, but being on the run for her life and that of their daughter had pushed her anger and sadness aside. Since he was no longer here to feel her anger, allowing it to continue to fester would serve no purpose other than to let it eat at her soul.

Lord, it's time I put the past firmly in the rearview mirror where it belongs. Please, help me let go of the anger I feel over my situation. Keep me and Rose—and Maxwell and Gus—safe through the night. I now realize it was reckless of me not to believe we really were in danger. The men Joe and Larry were involved with are truly evil and don't care that I don't know anything that can hurt them. I'm just a mom trying to do my best. When Marshal Ackerman relocates us, I will be more diligent in protecting this tiny life you've trusted in my care.

SIX

Maxwell rolled onto his back and sighed heavily. He had always had difficulty sleeping when he was on stakeout or protecting a witness. Even a twenty-minute catnap would help him be more alert if danger showed up on the doorstep. But it didn't matter how much he tried to tell himself that he needed rest, he could not quiet his brain enough to fall asleep. Pulling himself to a seated position, he picked up his cell phone off the coffee table and checked the time. 1:27 a.m.

No point lying on the couch, tossing and turning. It wouldn't accomplish anything other than to make him more irritated at his inability to sleep on command. Shoving his feet into his shoes, he crossed to the wooden pegs on the wall by the door and shrugged into his jacket. Even though he didn't expect the men to find them here, maybe he'd be able to sleep after he looked around outside. Ten minutes later, he'd checked the perimeter of the cabin, as well as the vacant property next door, and he'd carried in the remaining bags from Susan's SUV.

Taking off his coat, he rubbed his hands together and then blew on them. Maxwell wished he'd been able to go home and pack a bag before going on the run with his neighbor and her child. It would have been nice to have gloves and a change of clothes. He glanced at the small woodstove in the corner. The central heating unit was doing a sufficient job keeping the small cabin warm, but the weather forecaster had said the temperatures wouldn't reach above freezing for the next six days.

Tim kept a few clothes in a wardrobe in the attic. Maxwell had borrowed a raincoat when he'd stayed at the cabin last year. He would look through it in the morning to see if he could find gloves and warmer clothes. Then he'd bring firewood in from the shed. Best to be prepared in case they lost power.

The other concern would be food. He didn't imagine there would be much in the cupboards. Crossing to the kitchen, he checked the pantry. There were a few cans of soup, a couple of bags of dried beans and other staples like flour and sugar. Hopefully, additional snow would hold off until they could make it to the small locally owned grocery store about five miles away, but if not, at least they wouldn't starve.

Opening the cabinet beside the sink, he snagged a glass and filled it with cold water from the refrigerator dispenser. After he guzzled it, he placed the glass in the sink and settled onto a barstool at the small kitchen island. Then he pulled out his phone and began typing an email to his cousin.

Dear Tim, I had to use your rental cabin tonight. I'm sorry that I did so without asking permission first. It was a matter of life or death. Maxwell backspaced and deleted the last sentence. No need to get into any of the details. I'm sure you understand I would not have done so unless it was an urgent matter. I will transfer money to your account to cover the cost of the rental. Let me know if it is not enough, and I will transfer additional funds. He paused and read what he'd written. Maxwell had not seen his cousin, or any of the rest of the family, since moving to Maine, and he only spoke to his parents once a week. If he were being honest with himself, he wouldn't even do that if they didn't initiate the calls. Maybe it was time he reached out to those who cared for him. He and Tim had been close growing up, the closest thing to brothers either of them had had. No need to turn his back on the ones who hadn't turned theirs on him. Let me know the next time you're in Maine. I would really like to see you. He signed the email with his first name, then hit send.

Opening the financial app on his phone, he quickly transferred the promised funds to Tim's account.

"I thought I heard you moving around."

Susan stood at the edge of the hall, dressed as she had been earlier—minus shoes. That must have been how she had managed to sneak up on him.

"I'm sorry if I woke you."

She shrugged. "I'm a light sleeper. It's a side effect of being a single parent. When she needs me in the night, I have to respond. There's no one else to do it."

"I'm sorry." He didn't know what else to say. There would be no point pressing her about her past. The US Marshals Service had strict rules about participants in its Witness Protection Program remaining anonymous. If it hadn't been for his law enforcement training, he wouldn't have been able to guess she was in WITSEC.

"It is what it is. I don't mean to sound like I feel sorry for myself. I don't. I've always wanted to be a mom. I will do whatever is required, be whomever I have to be, to protect Rose. And I won't complain about it." She noticed the phone in his hand. "I'm sorry. Did I interrupt something?"

"No." Maxwell shook his head. "I sent my cousin an email explaining that I had to use the cabin for the night. And I was sending him money to cover the rental."

"Oh." She frowned. "If you tell me how much, I'll reimburse you for the cost."

"No need." He shoved his phone into his pocket. "I doubt there is any food in the refrigerator, but my cousin keeps a cabinet stocked with hot chocolate mixes, coffee, cookies and peanut butter crackers. Would you like a snack?"

"No. Thank you. I'm not hungry." She shook her head and settled onto the stool beside him. "You said you were an NYPD officer. Did you…" She pressed her lips together.

Please, don't let her ask why I left the force. I can't explain all of that, and I don't want to seem like I'm hiding something. But I am hiding something, aren't I? I'm hiding the fact that the people I thought were my closest friends, people I thought loved me, and the woman I was going to marry, all thought I was capable of deceit. That I, an officer of the law, was no better than a common criminal. Change the subject, now.

"Have you ever had issues reaching Marshal Ackerman in the past?"

"No. Never." Her voice wobbled and tears brimmed her eyes.

Not tears. He could handle almost anything, a stab wound, a fistfight—three against one— even his fiancée's betrayal. *Please, don't cry.*

"I'm sure it's nothing of concern. He's probably on an assignment somewhere." Whether or not Max believed his own words didn't matter. He only needed her to believe them. "How long have you been in the program?"

"Almost two years."

"And you've been in Fisher's Point this entire time?"

"Except for the first two weeks, yes."

"After all this time, I'm sure he wasn't expecting you to be found. So he may not have seen a need to let you know he was going to be away for a few days. You left him a voicemail. Maybe he'll call in the morning."

"With your experience of law enforcement, if you got called away on another assignment, would you leave a contact number for another officer with your protectee? Or would you just not let your protectee know that you are going to be unavailable?"

Maxwell knew exactly what she was getting at, and he agreed with her in theory. The marshal should have left her an alternative contact phone number. When someone was entrusted to an officer's care, the officer should never let their guard down. He suspected the marshal being unavailable was outside of his control. But Max would never say that to Susan. He would not add more stress to the load she was already carrying.

"Look, what I would or wouldn't do is of no importance here. I don't know what the protocol is for the Marshals Service. If you don't hear from him by tomorrow morning, we will figure out a game plan and go from there. Depending on our gut instinct, we may contact the closest Marshals office."

"If our gut instinct says don't…?"

"We may hide out here." He lifted both hands palms out and looked around the room, dimly lit by the hood vent light he had left on earlier for a night-light in case Susan woke up and needed to see where she was walking. "Tim won't care. In fact, I'm sure he would insist on it."

"Don't you have a job to get back to?"

"I work from home. The work will keep. But my conscience will not allow me to abandon you and your little girl."

"Thank you. For all you've done. I'm sure Marshal Ackerman will be in touch tomorrow, and you can go back to your life." She stood. "In the meantime, I'll return to bed so you can get some rest."

He watched as she walked away. "Good night, Susan."

Stopping in her tracks, she turned toward him. "My name is Brenda. Brenda Granger. If you're willing to put your life on the line to save a stranger and her child, you deserve to know her real name."

Before he could respond, she slipped into the bedroom and closed the door. His heart thudded in his chest. He hadn't expected her to tell him anything about her past, especially her name. It was a sign she trusted him, which was strangely gratifying considering people he'd known for over a decade had displayed zero trust in him.

Slipping his phone out of his pocket, he opened the web browser, navigated to a website dedicated to finding people and typed the name Brenda Granger. There were 137 women with that name in forty-one states. He would have to narrow it down by region. Brenda had a Southern accent. Age? He estimated her to be somewhere in her late twenties or early thirties.

He started scrolling through the results and then paused. *What are you doing? She trusts you enough to share her real name with you. She will fill in the other details tomorrow. Give her time.*

Placing his phone on the coffee table, he stretched out on the couch. In the morning, if she still couldn't reach Marshal Ackerman, he would probe her for more information. No matter what he had said, they couldn't hide out at the cabin indefinitely. But they needed to figure out who the men chasing her were before they ventured too far. Thankfully, the cabin was in a remote area and couldn't be traced to Susan—Brenda—so the men wouldn't find them there.

Why had she told him her real name? *Because he's kept you and Rose alive. Besides, if you can't reach Marshal Ackerman in the morning, you may have to continue to rely on Maxwell's law enforcement training to stay a step ahead of those men.*

A shiver shook her body. She hadn't spoken her real name aloud in almost two years. Brenda had been warned that if she didn't follow the guidelines—rule number one, don't reveal your true identity—she would be kicked out of the program. It was bad enough that she'd allowed Maxwell to guess that she was in WITSEC, but now she'd even told him her name. Marshal Ackerman was sure to be angry with her. He'd always been a fatherly type figure, guiding her and offering encouragement, and he had drilled it into her that she had to be Susan and never let her guard down.

She rolled over and wrapped her arm around Rose, pulling her close. "I love you, baby girl," she whispered softly. "I will do whatever it takes to keep you safe, even if it means sharing my true identity and past with a stranger."

Marshal Ackerman hadn't been there as a lifeline for her, like he'd promised to be, when she needed him most. Maxwell had. So for now, she would trust *him*. She was sure he'd have a lot of questions for her in the morning. He'd probably question her about the crime that landed her in the WITSEC program. Shame washed over her. Would he believe her innocence? And if he did, would he think she was naïve for trusting Joe and Larry so unconditionally?

Brenda puffed out a breath. She'd find out tomorrow. And what did she care if he thought badly of her? A lot, actually. Brenda had always been a rule follower. Breaking the rules was new to her. *Lord, I don't know why I did that. I kept a secret for twenty-two months. All I had to do was keep my mouth shut for another twelve hours or so. I could have taken him back to his house. No, I couldn't have done that. It's too far. But I could've driven him to a car rental place, and he could've figured out a way home. And Rose and I could've disappeared. Found a place to hide out until I could reach Marshal Ackerman.*

She knew very little about Maxwell Prescott, but she knew he wasn't likely to agree to letting her just disappear. Whether it was his sense of duty or something else that made him want to protect her and her child, she did not know, but she was thankful that he had been there this evening. Maybe that was why she trusted him with the truth.

Gus snored again, and she giggled. "Sleep well, furry friend."

There was sure to be a battle of wills when they had to part ways with the Australian shepherd. He had taken a liking to her child, and vice versa. Brenda imagined Rose would begin asking for a puppy now. Maybe, once they were settled some place new, she would give in and get a dog like Gus. Maxwell could help her pick one out. Tell her how to train it. No, that wouldn't happen. He would be back at his cabin, living his life. She was sure she could figure it out on her own. It was easy to find videos for everything on the internet. And she was pretty good at research. She rolled onto her side, wrapped her arm around Rose and pulled her closer, thankful that she and her daughter were safe and in a warm bed for what was left of the night.

Sometime later, barking followed by a scratching sound penetrated the foggy haze of sleep. What was wrong? Did the dog need to go out? Stretching her eyes wide, she tried to force herself to wake, just as she had all the times when Rose was a baby waking up through the night for a feeding. "It's okay, boy, I'll let you out."

The whimper turned to a growl, and she bolted upright. There was a knock on the bedroom door.

"I'm coming in," Maxwell announced as the door opened.

"Thanks for getting up to let him out." She yawned and laid back down.

"Wake up! That was not his *I need to go potty* bark. Someone's outside."

She jumped out of bed. "How can you be so sure?"

"Because I trained him, and I know his barks."

"Okay, what do we do?"

"You wait here. But stay alert. I'll take him and check outside. Gus, seek." The animal darted out of the room.

Brenda folded her arms around her stomach and stared after them. How could Earl and Jed have found them here? Surely it was just a squirrel or another wild animal that Gus heard. She crossed to close the door, and an icy breeze blew her hair. Gasping, she turned toward the window as the tall lanky man—the one called Jed—was climbing into the room, one hand outstretched toward her sleeping child.

"Maxwell! Help!" She dived toward the bed and threw her body on top of Rose.

A flying ball of fur hurdled through the air above her, and a piercing scream followed. Opening her eyes, she saw Gus, his teeth clamped into the man's arm.

"Go! Take Rose and hide." Maxwell's eyes

were focused on the scene playing out in front of them.

She didn't have to be told twice. Brenda scrambled off the bed, clutching a sobbing Rose to her chest, and stumbled out of the room. She raced into the bathroom, closed and locked the door behind her. For the second time that night, she lay in a stranger's bathtub with Rose, praying no bullets would hit them.

SEVEN

Maxwell holstered his weapon and rushed toward the window. Blood streamed down the intruder's arm. Time to get him inside and tied up. "Nice of you to join us here, Jed."

Shock registered in the other man's eyes, giving Max a brief moment of satisfaction.

"Release," Max commanded Gus.

The shepherd did as instructed, and Max reached for Jed's arm. Before he could connect, the bearded guy—Earl—appeared behind Jed, his gun drawn and aimed at Maxwell. The former police officer dove to the floor and palmed his own weapon. As he peeked over the mattress, Earl fired off a shot, barely missing him. Maxwell rapidly returned fire, directing his shots through the open window. The men dropped to the ground, disappearing from sight. Was Earl retreating that easily?

Maxwell waited a minute and listened. Then he army crawled over to the window and peered out. The full moon had dipped low on the horizon and the snow glistened, making the front yard eerily bright.

Jed was propped against the back bumper of an SUV parked behind Brenda's. Maxwell couldn't determine the make of the vehicle, but if the tires were any indication, it definitely had off-road capability. He watched as Earl rooted around in the back of the vehicle, his body mostly blocked by a balsam fir tree, making it impossible to get off a decent shot.

Max reached into his back pocket for his phone. The police wouldn't arrive quickly, but it couldn't hurt to have them headed their way, in case they were needed.

"Are they gone?" Brenda whispered from behind him.

He glanced at her. She was on her hands and knees in the hallway between the bedroom and bathroom, her head poking around the door.

"No. They're out front." He held up his phone. "I'm calling—"

"I tried to call 911. There's no cell service."

A quick look at his phone screen showed her words to be true. Shoving it back into his pocket, he peeked out the window. Earl had knelt beside Jed, using the injured man for cover, and was in the process of wrapping some kind of cloth around Jed's arm. While it looked like he was distracted by his injured friend, Max knew Earl was preparing for a second attack. Otherwise, he would have loaded Jed into the vehicle and made an escape.

"Get yours and Rose's coats and shoes and that carrier thing you wore. I left it on the coffee table. Be prepared…for anything. If we have to make a run for it, chances are we'll have to do it on foot. Through the woods."

She crawled into the room and snagged the backpack that held toddler supplies then, without a word, turned around and disappeared from sight. He heard her hurry along the short hall and move around in the living area, doing as he'd instructed.

Hopefully, if they had to flee the cabin, Brenda and Rose would be better protected against the elements than they had been when they showed up on his doorstep. Always prepared, Maxwell had left his boots on when he lay down, so the only thing he would need to grab on the way out was his jacket. And he'd be fine.

Maxwell turned his focus back to the men outside. He needed to keep eyes on them so Earl couldn't get the jump on him. The bearded man had moved to the opposite side of the vehicle and was leaned inside, searching for something. The overhead light was off, so Max couldn't see what he was doing. Earl straightened—the

SUV blocking his body. What was he holding? It appeared to be a slender-necked bottle. Was he drinking?

Goose bumps popped out on the back of Max's neck. He watched as the man twisted the top off the bottle and took a long swig, then took a torn strip of cloth and pushed one end of it into the container. No! He was making a Molotov cocktail.

Max raised his weapon, centering the man's head in his sights. He'd much rather take the man alive, but he could not let him light the incendiary device. Max pulled the trigger at the same instant Earl dropped something—possibly a lighter—and bent down, causing the bullet to miss its target. Frustration welled inside him.

"Gus, guard!" He knew his K9 partner would protect the woman and child in his stead. "Go, now!" he added for Brenda's benefit.

The bathroom door squeaked open, and footsteps raced through the small cabin and out the back door. Then there was silence. Turning back to the window, he caught sight of a tiny, flickering flame reflecting on the window of the shooter's vehicle. The small flame ignited into a larger one. Earl had lit the cloth wick. Focusing on the flame, he aimed his weapon and followed its movement as it rose higher. Rising with the lit Molotov cocktail in his hand, Earl took a step to his right, drew back and threw. Max pulled the trigger.

Everything seemed to move in slow motion. Maxwell's bullet connected with its target—hitting Earl in the left shoulder—as the combustible bottle glided through the air, headed straight toward Max. He dove toward the door. The bottle hit the bed and burst into flames, heat engulfing the room instantly. Staying low, he crawled out of the room, pushed to his feet and ran down the hall and out the open sliding door. He took several deep breaths—the cold air burning his lungs. Two sets of footprints—one human and one canine—made a trail through the snow and into the woods.

He'd take care of the men and then follow the footprints to locate Gus and his charges. Bounding down the deck steps, he wished he'd grabbed his jacket, but no matter. With both men injured, it shouldn't take him long to subdue them and tie them up. Then he would find Brenda and Rose and figure out how to call in the fire.

A gunshot rang out, and a bullet whizzed past his head. He spun around and returned fire. Earl ducked behind the corner of the house. Maxwell walked backward while continuing to shoot, not giving the other man a chance to get off a shot. *Click*. His gun dry fired. He pulled the trigger again. *Click*. He was out of bullets. And his extra magazine was at home in a locked box on the top shelf of his closet. Earl poked his head out. Maxwell turned and charged into the woods. A bullet hit an aspen tree to his right, and he plowed deeper into the thicket of trees. *Lord, I know I haven't come to you in a long time, but I pray Earl's injury slows him down. I beg of you, let me reach Brenda and Rose and get them safely out of the woods before they're shot or succumb to frostbite.*

Another gunshot boomed. Brenda flinched. Pulling the plaid wool throw she'd grabbed off the couch as she'd ran out of the cabin tighter around her daughter's tiny body, she prayed. "Lord, please, don't let them find us."

She had taken shelter behind a large boulder once the cabin was no longer in sight, so she could catch her breath. Grandpa Henry's rifle, which she'd remembered to grab on the way out, was leaned beside her. The moon had sunk below the mountain, and she knew it wouldn't be long before the sun rose. Which meant she needed to get moving again. Even though she'd known the killers could track her footsteps, she'd felt somewhat safe in the dark. However, the forest in winter wouldn't provide the coverage it would have in the summer, and once the sun rose, the men could spot her from a distance, no longer needing to rely on following prints in the snow.

"Okay, baby girl." She kissed the top of Rose's curly head, regretting she hadn't remembered to grab her knit cap off the bedside table. "We've got to get moving again. Remember we're playing a game of hide-and-seek. So, stay really quiet. Okay?"

Rose looked at her with the same wide-eyed expression she'd worn for most of the last eight hours, her thumb shoved in her mouth, and nodded.

"Okay, Gus, let's go." Grasping a small tree, she pulled herself to her feet. She hadn't felt this wobbly since the end of her pregnancy. The combination of snow that covered tops of her boots and the weight of her daughter being carried in the front made her steps clumsy.

The Australian shepherd trotted over to her, looking from Rose to Brenda and back again. It was almost as if he could read her mind. "Nope. I will not transfer her to my back." Brenda wasn't sure if she was trying to convince the dog or herself. "She's safer and warmer right where she is."

Resolutely, she grasped the barrel of the rifle and started walking deeper into the woods. *Lord, I have no clue where I am. I don't know if I'm walking toward help or farther away, but I trust you to guide my steps and lead me and my daughter to safety.*

Sometime later, as the gray dawn of morning blanketed the area, she paused and took in her surroundings. The sound of a bubbling stream echoed in the morning silence. It suddenly hit her she hadn't heard a gunshot in at least ten minutes. Did that mean the men had left? Or had they killed Maxwell and were tracking her through the woods? The smell of smoke crinkled her nose. Firewood? Excitement surged in her. Maybe there was a house close by. She turned in a circle, searching the horizon. A big plume of smoke rose in the sky from the direction of the cabin. That wasn't smoke from a chimney. It was a house fire. Turning, she darted through the trees. She broke through the tree line and stepped out onto a creek bank. The stream was roughly fifteen feet wide, the water in the center flowing steadily, while the water at the edge had formed a frozen crust on either side of it.

Snap. A twig broke behind her. She glanced over her shoulder.

The dark shadow of a man was headed straight toward her. There was no place to hide. Clutching the rifle, she looked left, and then right, desperate for an escape.

"Don't shoot! It's me."

Gus bounded toward the figure, his tail wagging.

Relief washed over her as Maxwell came into view. Her heart pounded in her chest. Brenda's knees suddenly felt incapable of holding her up.

Maxwell rushed to her side and grasped her upper arms. "Are you alright? Do you need to sit down? I didn't mean to frighten you."

"No. I'm..."

He guided her to a fallen log and dusted off the snow with his bare hands. Then he helped her to sit.

"Mash found us."

"Yes, I did."

He grinned at Rose, and she giggled. Brenda's heart skipped a beat. She'd never seen her daughter interact with any man other than the elderly men at church. *How many father-daughter moments had Rose been robbed of because of Joe's decision to take part in illegal activities?* And now, since Joe had been murdered in prison, Rose would never even have the chance to meet him. Which was of no concern if they weren't able to escape the men after them because they'd all be dead. Fear gripped Brenda and she trembled.

Maxwell sank onto the log beside her, pulled

her into his arms and rubbed his hands up and down her back.

"My can't breathe," Rose declared, squirming to be free.

The declaration was like a jolt of awareness, waking Brenda from a fog. She pulled back and met Maxwell's gaze. "Thank you, but I'm fine."

"I was afraid you were going into shock." He shoved his hand through his hair as she'd seen him do several times. "Sorry if I overstepped."

"No. I appreciate your concern. It's just—" She released a slow breath, a puff of fog floating into the air. "What do we do now? Where are the men? And is your cousin's cabin on fire?"

"Now, we find our way out of these woods. I'm not sure where the men are, but they're both injured, so I don't think they'll make it far if they try to follow us." He sighed. "And, yes, the cabin is on fire. I imagine someone has seen the smoke and called it in to the fire department by now."

"Do you think the men are still at the cabin? Should we go back and get my vehicle?"

"We are over a mile from the cabin by now. If we follow the stream, it should lead us to the road. There's a small bridge about two miles east of the cabin. I'm sure this is the water it crosses. So the best thing to do is try to find the road and see if we can flag down a car to drive us into town."

Her eyes widened. "We're just going to abandon my vehicle?"

"Your SUV was parked right by the front steps. I imagine it's been damaged in the fire. I'm sorry."

"But…what…"

She may not have been in shock earlier, but if he didn't get her someplace warm soon, she likely would be at risk of both shock and hypothermia.

He pulled her to her feet, taking in the weary expression in her blue eyes and noting the dark circles. "Give me Rose."

She tightened her grip on the little girl. "It's okay. I've got her."

"You're exhausted. We'll make it out of here faster if you aren't struggling with the burden of carrying her."

"My child isn't a burden."

The little girl looked from her mother to him, and back again, as if she knew the discussion was about her. She was an inquisitive child. He smiled. Since moving to Maine, he'd missed even more of his nieces' and nephew's lives. He had no idea what their interests were. Maybe it was time he went home for a short visit. But first he had to get out of these woods and get Brenda and Rose to safety.

"Poor choice of words. I know she's not a burden. No child is." He shoved a hand through his hair—a habit he'd developed since he'd stopped keeping it in a crew cut.

"Thank you. I appreciate the offer, but Rose takes a while to warm up to strangers. It would be easier for me to keep carrying her than it would be to fight to get her to allow you to carry her." Her eyes narrowed as if she were taking in his appearance for the first time. "Where's your coat?" she asked in an accusatory mom voice.

He shrugged. "Didn't have time to grab it."

She started removing the blanket she had wrapped around Rose. "Here. Take this."

"No. I can't. Keep it for Rose."

"She'll be fine. She has on her coat and mittens." Brenda looked at his hands. "You don't even have gloves."

Maybe he could use this as a bargaining tool to get her to allow him to carry the child and take some of the weight off her shoulders, literally and figuratively. "I'll only accept the blanket if I can carry Rose and we share it."

"I don't know..."

Rose pulled her thumb out of her mouth with a plopping sound. Then she stretched out her arms toward Maxwell. Brenda's eyes widened. She unfastened the straps holding Rose in the carrier and allowed him to lift her out of it.

"Guess I was wrong." Brenda slipped the carrier off her shoulders and loosened the straps so they would fit around his waist. "I've been doing a front carry so she's somewhat protected from bullets."

"Jed and Earl were both injured. I haven't seen them following me, and it they come anywhere near us Gus will alert. So, I'll carry her on my back, if you don't mind."

"Okay." She trusted him to protect Rose, but she would try to walk behind him as much as possible. If either Jed or Earl showed up, she'd use her own body to shield her child.

Once Rose was firmly fastened into the carrier, Brenda draped the blanket around her and him. When he tried to push the blanket off his shoulders, Brenda grasped the ends, pulled them around front and tied them loosely.

"This was the deal. You and Rose *share* the blanket." She looked up at him. Her strawberry-blond hair framed her heart-shaped face, and a smile lit up her eyes.

The sudden urge to pull her close and wrap his arms around her hit him like a freight train going seventy miles an hour. Fighting the desire, he forced himself to take a step backward. "Uh…are you sure…she won't feel too…uh…confined?"

In an instant, the smile was wiped from her

face. Regret washed over him, but there was no undoing it now. He couldn't tell her he'd felt a moment of attraction to her. As far as he knew, she was a married woman. And even if she wasn't, he couldn't take the risk of having his heart broken again. He'd learned the hard way that someone's declaration of undying love didn't automatically equate to their unbreakable trust. Sometimes, he wondered how different his life would have turned out if Ellen had believed in him and had stood by his side as he faced the accusations of the department.

"Maxwell... Max..." Brenda shook his arm.

"What?" He frowned and turned to her.

Her brow furrowed. "Where were you just now? It seemed like your mind wandered off."

"Sorry." Time to focus on the task at hand. He could fight the dark memories of the past when he didn't have people depending on him. "We need to get moving."

Rose babbled incoherent words, and Brenda smiled. "I'd say my daughter agrees with you."

He guided the way, helping Brenda across fallen logs and around large rocks that blocked their way. Gus trudged along beside them. Maxwell regretted he hadn't put Gus's winter gear on him before they left his house last evening so that he would have stayed warmer. Hindsight would always be twenty-twenty. It was best not to focus on what he should have done but rather on what he could do in the here and now.

"Do you want to tell me how a young woman from…?"

"North Carolina."

"North Carolina." He smiled. "I thought I detected a Southern accent."

"Yeah, I've tried to lose it, but so far I haven't been able to."

"It seems to be more pronounced when you're excited or scared. I noticed it when you showed up at my house, but then when you were speaking to the police at your house, it was barely detectible."

"Thanks." She shrugged. "I guess you're wanting to know a little about my background?"

"It might be helpful in figuring out who's after you, since you said you didn't know."

"I know the why. I don't know the who."

He waited, giving her time to decide what he should or shouldn't know. He'd learned long ago to read the demeanor of the person he was interrogating. Sometimes, they simply needed a little space, so they'd feel in control of the situation, then they'd share everything they knew freely.

After a few minutes of walking in silence, she sighed. "My husband—late husband—Joe was murdered in prison a few months ago—"

"I'm sorry."

"Doesn't matter. I mean I mourn his death and the life we should have had together, but the marriage was fractured when he was arrested for murder and trafficking drugs. Then I discovered he'd had an affair while I was pregnant, and it destroyed any remaining love I felt for him."

He stopped in his tracks. How could any man cheat on the woman in front of him? She was not only beautiful, but she was also a strong, independent woman who loved her child deeply. Maxwell had no doubt she'd been devoted to her husband and her marriage.

Brenda paused beside him, one eyebrow raised questioningly.

"If Joe was the one running drugs, why would his associates be after you? Did you see anything that would connect you to them?" He started walking again, and she fell into step beside him.

"No, but my brother was involved, too. They used our family auto repair shop as a cover, hiding drugs in the tires they put on vehicles that the people—or person—running the drug ring sent to the shop." She furrowed her brow. "I always thought it odd how many cars with out of state tags purchased tires from our shop. Guess now I know why."

He had so many questions, but they would wait. For now.

As the first streaks of sunrise painted the sky

with yellow, orange and purple, they reached a waterfall that stood about ten feet high, ice coating the edges. The bank on either side had narrowed, and there wasn't a defined trail. He rested against a tree and examined the situation.

Brenda stepped behind him and checked on Rose.

"How is she?"

"Sleeping, like a baby," she answered softly. "Of course, she *is* a baby, or at least, she's still one to me. I just hope this experience doesn't become a permanent memory for her."

"I'm sure it won't. You'll make lots of happy memories together. Those memories will help push this one into the farther recesses of her brain until it's long forgotten." He straightened. "Going up this incline is going to be slippery. Hang on to me."

She shook her head vehemently. "Can't do that. I don't want to make you trip and injure Rose. You get my daughter safely to the top, and I'll worry about getting myself up there."

Maxwell wanted to argue, but he'd witnessed her stubborn determination several times already. He knew there would be no changing her mind. "Do you want to lead the way? Or would you rather follow?"

"I'll follow. That way, I'll see where to step."

With a slight nod, he turned and picked his

way up the incline. When he reached the top, his breathing was labored and his back was sweaty. Maxwell was thankful she'd allowed him to carry Rose. He wasn't sure Brenda would have been able to climb the difficult terrain while balancing the added weight of the child.

Turning, he held out a hand and helped her up the last steep part. The combination of the stiff wind and exercise had given her cheeks a rosy tint. "Are you okay? Do you need to sit for a moment and catch your breath?"

"No." She puffed out a breath. "I'd rather keep moving if that's alright. We may need to go slow for a few minutes, but that will still be better than stopping completely."

"If you're sure."

"I am." She tucked her hands into her jacket pockets, a determined expression on her face. "Lead the way."

A quarter of a mile farther along the trail, Gus froze and released a low growl. Spotting what had caused the K9 to alert, Maxwell stopped short and Brenda bumped into him. Turning, he put his finger to his lips. "Shhh."

He pointed at a large elk drinking from the stream.

"Oh, he's beautiful," Brenda whispered, and edged past Max for a better look at the bull elk—his antlers displaying fourteen points.

Maxwell put a firm hand on her shoulder. "Stay back. They can be aggressive toward people."

She shrank against his side. "He's blocking our path. What do we do?"

"Stand still and hope—"

The elk lifted his head and glared at them. Locked in a staring contest with the animal, Max uttered a command under his breath for Gus to stand down. The elk released a loud shriek, and then sprinted into the woods, out of sight. *Thank You, Lord.*

"That was close," Brenda sighed.

"Too close."

The sound of a vehicle penetrated the calm morning, and hope surged inside him. "Sounds like we're close to the road. Let's keep moving."

Soon, the bridge came into view. Relief and dread collided in his stomach. *Dear Lord, please, let a friendly person who doesn't ask too many questions stop and offer us a ride. I pray Jed and Earl are long gone.*

Brenda clutched his arm. "What if the shooters are waiting for us? They have to know we'd make our way to the road."

He reached behind his back and held on to Rose. Then, using his free hand, he unclipped the waist belt of the harness. "You stay hidden in the trees with Rose and Gus. I'll flag down a vehicle and make sure it's safe before you come out of the woods."

"Do you think anyone will give us a ride after they see the rifle?"

"Yes. I'll explain we had car trouble on one of the lesser traveled side roads. My hunting rifle was in the vehicle, so I brought it in case we encountered a wild animal that wanted to attack."

"Okay."

With her assistance, he shrugged out of the carrier. Then he helped her put it on, in the front carrying position. Rose squirmed and fussed as he worked to tighten all the straps on the carrier. Brenda patted her daughter's bottom and whispered words of comfort in her ear. She was a wonderful mother. Protectiveness welled inside him. He didn't know what all she'd been through, but he knew she and Rose deserved to live a long and happy life. Once they made it to a warm, dry location, he would call the Marshals Service himself to see why Brenda and Rose had been abandoned by their handler. He might just have to have a few words with the man about responsibility and duty.

EIGHT

"...been walking for miles...encountered an elk but he left us alone."

Brenda gathered bits and pieces of the story Maxwell was giving the driver of the red pickup truck that had stopped to offer help. The driver must have believed the story, because Max motioned for her to come out of hiding.

Gus walked in front of her, his tail wagging. The weight of the situation instantly lifted. The animal had powerful instincts. If the man in the vehicle was dangerous, he'd know it and never let Rose inside.

"I really appreciate this," Maxwell said to the driver. He turned and met her eyes. "Honey, this is Walt. He's going to give us a ride to the diner. We'll be able to call a tow truck from there."

Honey? It seemed they were pretending to be a family. She'd go along with it if it meant keeping Rose safe.

Brenda peered inside the vehicle. An elderly

gentleman with white hair and bright blue eyes smiled at her. "Your husband told me what happened. I'm sorry you've had such difficulties on your vacation, missus. You and that little one hop on in. I've got the heat cranked up. Won't take long for you to unthaw."

Brenda met Maxwell's gaze and raised an eyebrow. *Husband?*

He shrugged as if reading her thoughts. Then he opened the back door and commanded Gus inside. After Gus settled on the floorboard, she moved to enter, but he halted her. "I'll go first," he whispered.

She stepped back, puzzled. Why wouldn't he let her inside first? Though she had known him for less than twenty-four hours, she'd never known him not to be a gentleman. She'd have to ask him later when they were alone. Once he was settled, she slid inside and closed the door.

"I'll drive once everyone is fastened. As you discovered, we can't take chances in these road conditions." Walt turned to look back at them and frowned. "I'd prefer it if you had a car seat for the little one, but I guess that can't be helped."

"She should be safe in this carrier since she's strapped to me." Brenda tightened her hold on Rose, who had awakened. Brenda frowned. "Though I'm not sure how I can wear a seat belt. I wouldn't want the shoulder strap to hurt her."

"Scoot closer to me. The middle belt is just a lap belt," Maxwell told her.

She complied, and Gus moved to give her room for her feet. Once she was fastened, Max put his arm around her shoulders and drew her close.

Walt smiled, turned around and pulled onto the highway. "Where did you say the accident happened? I didn't see any vehicles on the side of the road as I came through."

"It was a side road. Runs parallel to this one. Hadn't seen any other cars on it, so I thought we'd catch a ride faster if we hiked through the woods to a road with more traffic." Maxwell kissed the top of Brenda's head. "It was a long hike. Wasn't it, honey?"

"Uh-huh." She leaned her head on his shoulder. "We really appreciate the hospitality, Walt."

"My pleasure. Actually, this happens a lot around here. Well, I've never found an entire family and a dog stranded on the side of the road, but I usually pick up someone who experienced some type of car trouble at least once a month. It's part of living in a wilderness area." He began to hum a tune, and the conversation stopped.

By the time they reached the small town, Brenda's hands and feet had started to thaw, and Rose was awake and babbling to Gus. Walt turned into a crowded parking lot and pulled to a stop close to a door with the words The Daily Grind Diner painted on it in red block letters. "Well, folks, this is the best diner in town. You can't beat their coffee." He turned and looked at her. "You have a beautiful family. Cherish it."

Tears welled in her eyes, and her throat tightened. God had blessed her with a beautiful daughter, but she did not and would never have the family Walt thought she had, complete with a husband and a dog.

Maxwell unfastened his seat belt and leaned forward with his hand outstretched. "Thank you, sir." He and Walt shook hands. "Would you come inside and allow me to buy you breakfast?"

"No need." The older man shook his head. "I've already had breakfast. I'll just head over to the hardware store and then be on my way back home."

Brenda opened her door, and Gus hopped out. Then she exited the vehicle, with Maxwell right behind her.

Walt rolled down the passenger side window and met her eyes. "Don't take your blessings for granted." Without waiting for a reply, he waved, put his truck in gear and pulled off.

"That was strange. Why would he say that to me, specifically? He doesn't know me," she wondered aloud.

"I'm sure he wasn't trying to single you out

and meant it for us both." Maxwell opened the door to the diner, and a bell overhead dinged.

"Sit anywhere folks. I'll be right with you," a waitress with red hair—wearing a pair of blue jeans and a blue T-shirt with the The Daily Grind Diner logo on the back—yelled over her shoulder as she carried a tray of food to a table near them.

"It's cold outside. Is it okay if my dog sits here in the foyer," Maxwell asked. "He'll stay out of the way and won't be a bother."

"Sure, honey. As long as he doesn't bother anyone."

"Gus, stay." Maxwell pointed to a spot in the corner. Gus walked over and sat on the other side of a potted plant.

The place was bustling. There was only one table and a booth empty. Thankfully, the tables had been arranged in a manner that provided maximum space between them for walking.

"Follow me." Maxwell snagged a child's booster seat from a nearby stand and headed to the booth. No one even blinked at the rifle he held in his hand. Reaching the booth, he placed the booster seat on one side of the table and turned to take Rose.

Brenda looked around and spotted a sign pointing the way to the restrooms. "I need to take her to the restroom."

"Okay, I'll walk with you."

"No. We'll be fine." She leaned in close. "If I need you, I'll scream."

Five minutes later, Brenda returned to the table with a dry, and happy, Rose. Her daughter had used the *big girl potty* and had insisted on putting on a pair of her *big girl panties*, refusing to put on the diaper that Brenda had wanted her to wear. It had been four months since Rose had worn a diaper during the daytime, only wearing one at night because she was still prone to accidents. Brenda didn't know how readily available restrooms would be while on the run from killers. However, as a mom, she'd learned to pick her battles, and forcing her child to wear a diaper was not a battle she wanted to have at the moment. A happy Rose would be easier to handle than a cranky, whiny Rose.

"Sorry that took so long." She slid into the booth and settled Rose into the booster seat.

"Everything okay?" Maxwell smiled at Rose who was busy trying to open a small packet of crayons so she could draw on the child's paper place mat.

"Yes. I just have a strong-willed daughter." She opened a small tub of creamer and dumped it into the steaming cup of coffee that sat in front of her. "Thank you for ordering coffee for me."

"You're welcome." He took a sip from his own cup of dark brew. "I wasn't sure what you or

Rose would like to eat, so I asked the waitress to give us a few minutes."

She scanned the menu and placed their orders when their waitress Caitlyn returned a few minutes later. Soon, the table was laden with scrambled eggs, bacon and pancakes.

"While you were in the restroom, I asked the waitress if there were any car rental places or taxies in the area." Maxwell used the side of his fork to cut off a bite of his blueberry pancake. "She said the closest rental place is in Windham, twenty miles away. But Jimmy—the brown-haired guy sitting alone in the corner—will drive elderly members of the community to nearby towns when he has time."

She turned and peered at the man in question. He appeared to be in his mid-to late thirties. Dressed in a flannel shirt and boots, he could have been the lumberjack poster boy for a logging company. "Do you think he'll drive us? We're not from the community, and we're far from elderly."

"Caitlyn said she'd tell him about our situation and see what he said." Maxwell took another bite of pancake.

"Do you think it's wise for us to involve other people in our…situation? What if Jed and Earl track us?" She'd already put one innocent person's life in danger. She was hesitant to involve anyone else.

Placing his fork on his plate, Maxwell picked up a napkin and wiped his mouth. Then he propped his elbows on the table and leaned close to her. "I don't think they'll be able to find us now. I've been pondering how they tracked us to the cabin. I think they may have put a tracker on your vehicle before we returned to your house."

"But there was no sign of them when we got there."

"I'm sure they were hiding somewhere nearby, and once the police left, they saw their chance to attack again."

"Okay, but what do we do if Jimmy can't drive us?"

"If he can't, or won't, drive us, we'll figure something else out."

They finished their meal, and Caitlyn brought the check. Maxwell took out his wallet as Brenda cleaned Rose's face with a wet disposable wipe. A shadow fell across the table, and Brenda looked up.

Jimmy stood towering above them. "Caitlyn said you folks ran into some trouble and need a ride to Windham. I have ninety minutes free, which gives me just enough time for the round-trip journey, but only if you can be ready to go in five minutes."

"We're ready now." Maxwell dropped the money on the table. "Did she also tell you I have a dog?"

"Saw him when you came in. He's well trained. Hasn't moved since you arrived. He can come, too." Jimmy narrowed his eyes at Rose. "Do you have a car seat for her?"

Brenda's chest tightened. Would he deny them a ride without a car seat? She'd never let her child ride without one if it could be helped. "No, I—"

"We had to walk and weren't able to carry it." Maxwell slid out of the booth and stood. "If there's a store or consignment shop nearby, I'm happy to buy one. We need it for our journey, anyway."

"Doubt you'd find one around here. If you did, it would take too long, and I wouldn't have time to drive you." Jimmy scratched his cheek, then grabbed their check and money off the table. "Gimme a minute."

He walked over to the cash register where Caitlyn waited and handed her the money. Brenda scrambled out of the booth and stood beside Maxwell. "He's an interesting character."

"Yep."

Jimmy smiled and motioned for them. Caitlyn disappeared into the kitchen as they walked over. "Caitlyn said you can borrow her son's car seat, since I can return it before she gets off work. We'll meet her out back. Come on."

Brenda's heart swelled. She'd always heard stories about how people in other parts of the country weren't as friendly to strangers as people in the South. She had no clue how such an untrue rumor had gotten started because she'd received nothing but kindness from everyone she'd met.

Thank You, Lord, for putting good people in our path to help us along the way. I pray Maxwell is right and Jed and Earl won't be able to trail us, but if they do, please, keep the ones helping us safe from harm. Amen.

"You folks wouldn't know anything about the cabin fire on Sunny Ridge Road this morning, would you?" Jimmy asked casually, as they pulled out of the parking lot.

Maxwell heard Brenda's soft gasp from the back seat. He turned and met her gaze, giving a slight shake of his head. Then he looked at the man driving. Would he take them straight to the police department? Would they be arrested for breaking and entering and leaving the scene of a fire? It was imperative to Brenda's safety that her name and photo not appear on an inmate list on some police station's website. "Why would you ask that?"

"I'm a volunteer firefighter. Worked the call."

"Still doesn't explain why you would ask us about it. Was there anything at the scene to connect us to the fire?" Different scenarios raced through Max's mind. Would Jimmy allow him to turn himself in but let Brenda and Rose to go free? After all, it had been his idea to take refuge at his cousin's cabin. Brenda had no responsibility in the matter.

"I'm not accusing you of anything. Just asking." Jimmy stopped at a four-way stop, then turned right, headed out of town.

Answer without being defensive. See how it plays out. Worst-case scenario, you blow Brenda's cover and insist the local law enforcement contact the Marshals Service. Maybe that would be the best option. Brenda and Rose would be in temporary police custody until someone from the Marshals showed up to collect them. They'd be safe. Unless there was a corrupt cop running things in this small town. Brenda had said her husband and brother had been mixed up with a drug ring. Without knowing who was running the ring, he had no way of knowing how far it spread. It wouldn't be unheard-of for it to reach across multiple states, or even multiple countries. And she'd said people that had purchased tires from her family's auto repair shop had driven vehicles with tags from other states. Had any of them been from Maine?

"Look, you might as well come clean. I know the owner of that cabin. I know he's out of town and didn't have any renters scheduled to be there this week. Also, there was an SUV left on scene—registered to Susan Warner—a car seat inside."

Maxwell looked at the man's profile. "Then why aren't you taking us to the police station?"

"Because I want to hear your story. I texted Tim after we extinguished the fire. He said he'd gotten an email from his cousin—a former NYPD officer—telling him he was staying the night at the cabin. Said his cousin also transferred funds to his account to cover the cost of the night."

"Yeah, guess I owe him a lot more now."

"I would say so." Jimmy spared a quick glance in Maxwell's direction before turning his gaze back to the road. "Tim said if you had taken refuge at his cabin, especially with a woman and child, it was because you had no other choice."

Brenda leaned forward, placing a hand on the back of Maxwell's seat. "We didn't. Mine and my daughter's lives—"

"*Susan* escaped an abusive relationship. She's been in hiding, trying to raise her daughter away from the abuse." Maxwell shifted in his seat and placed a hand on hers. Squeezing lightly, he met her gaze. *Let me handle this*, he pleaded with his eyes.

She nodded and leaned back.

"What kind of person would set fire to the cabin where a child slept?" Jimmy asked incredulously.

"The person we're running from," Maxwell stated. "Did you notice the bullet hole in the back window of the vehicle? It barely missed the child."

"He did that with her inside?"

Max nodded. "Yes. Susan and I are neighbors. She showed up at my home last night frightened. I couldn't let her take off in the middle of the night, alone with a child, so I was going to drive her to a hotel. But we were followed. After we escaped, I decided to hideout at Tim's cabin. I knew he wouldn't mind."

Silence engulfed the cab of the pickup truck, and the heavy weight of dread settled on Max's shoulders. Rose babbled happily in the back seat, having what seemed to be a very important conversation with Gus. Her innocence was a small ray of sunshine in this dreary situation. He prayed he could keep her, and her beautiful mom, safe.

"You're former NYPD, but you don't trust the police, do you?"

"Not really, Jimmy." He couldn't admit to the stranger driving them that Brenda was in WITSEC and her cover would be blown if they went to the police. Would his own distrust of his fellow law enforcement officers be the key to getting the man to keep their identity a secret? "While most men and women in law enforcement are decent, God-fearing people, I've encountered some of the most corrupt in the business. I can't take a chance with Susan's and her child's lives. If the person after her showed up and offered the wrong officer a pocket full of money…"

Jimmy slowed and activated his turn signal. "Then you need to thank Tim. He told my boss the car belonged to a friend of his family and he'd given her permission to leave it there for a few days. Said he'd notify her of the fire and have her contact her insurance company to pick up her vehicle."

"So it was damaged?" Brenda asked from the back seat.

"Afraid so." Jimmy turned into the parking lot of the rental car company. "Beyond repair."

He pulled into a parking space and put the vehicle into Park, then he turned and looked at Brenda. "I will pray for yours and your little one's safety. My sister escaped an abusive relationship. No woman should have to live in fear."

"Thank you," Brenda replied softly. "And thank you for driving us here."

Maxwell dug out his wallet. "Let me give you gas money."

"No. Put that away." Jimmy waved his hand. "I'm glad I could help. Just keep them safe. And call your cousin when you get a chance, so he doesn't worry."

"I will. Thank you." Max held out his hand.

Jimmy accepted the handshake, then tightened his grip slightly, and leaned in. "The corrupt cops win when the good cops give up the fight."

Maxwell's throat tightened. Pressing his lips together, he gave a slight nod. Then he climbed out of the vehicle and ushered Brenda, Rose and Gus into the rental car office. Resolve washed over him. After renting a vehicle, he'd drive Brenda and Rose to the nearest Marshals office. They would take over her protection, and he and Gus could return home. Or maybe he'd go visit his parents. He had skipped the family Christmas gathering this year, choosing to remain in Maine where he could sulk alone.

But a family reunion wouldn't happen until he safely handed his charges over to the US Marshals Service.

NINE

Brenda settled Rose into the car seat Maxwell had rented along with the midsize SUV. The money he'd spent to keep her and Rose safe was adding up. She didn't know how she'd ever repay him, but she would, even if it took her years to do so. Of course, she'd have to figure out a way to send the money so it couldn't be traced to her or the US Marshals Service would definitely kick her out of the program. And if she'd learned nothing else in the past twelve hours, she'd learned that her life was indeed in danger. She wasn't sure how she'd slipped up and given away her location, but when she got to a new home with a new identity, she'd be extra careful, maybe be more of a recluse like Maxwell.

Climbing into the front seat, she pulled her cell phone out of her pocket. Fifteen percent battery life. "I'll try to call Marshal Ackerman again. Do you think we can stop somewhere

where I can pick up a phone charger and a few items for Rose?"

"Sure." Maxwell pulled up the navigation system and searched for a department store. Selecting a big box store located three miles away, he activated the directions. Then he backed out of the parking lot.

Brenda pulled up Marshal Ackerman's phone number—saved in her phone as Uncle Ace—and pressed Call. The call was answered on the second ring by an unfamiliar female voice. "Ms. Warner, is everything okay?"

"Who is this?" Brenda placed the call on speaker so Maxwell could listen.

"My name is Marshal Henderson," the woman replied.

"Where's Marshal Ackerman?"

"He's...indisposed." There was whispering in the background. "Where are you? We've been looking for you."

Maxwell reached over and hit the mute button on the phone. "Do you know this woman?"

"No."

"Marshal Ackerman has never mentioned her?"

She shook her head. "Do you think she's really a marshal?" Brenda's chest tightened, and she gasped. "Do you think they—"

"Ms. Warner. Answer me. Where are you? I'll send someone to pick you up."

"Tell her you'll call her back," Maxwell said.

Brenda unmuted the phone. "Sorry. I'll call back."

"Wait. Tell—"

She disconnected the call.

"Power off your phone," Maxwell commanded.

Her phone rang, and *Uncle Ace* flashed on the screen. She immediately sent the call to voicemail and shut down the device, as Maxwell had instructed. "Okay, it's off, but why?"

"A woman you've never heard of answered the phone that belongs to your handler. She wouldn't tell you where he was, *and* someone was whispering to her in the background. Also, she said they'd been looking for you, but you don't have any missed calls." He pulled into the parking lot of the big box store and parked as close to the entrance as he could. Then he turned to her. "Marshal Henderson may be legit, but we've had too many close calls, so I'd rather not take a chance. I'll drive you to the US Marshals Service office in Portland. They can verify if there's a Marshal Henderson or not. And, hopefully, tell us what happened to Marshal Ackerman."

"I trust your instincts, so if that's what you think we should do, I'm fine with the plan." Without Maxwell, she and Rose would most likely already be dead. There was no way she could ever thank him for all he'd done, but as long as he was willing to stay by their side, she would happily accept any advice he offered.

He opened his door. "Let's be quick."

He didn't have to tell her twice. She bounded out of the vehicle, opened the back door and started unfastening Rose.

"Do you want the carrier?" Maxwell asked as he leaned in on the other side and petted Gus.

"No. Getting her in and out of it will slow us down."

"Okay." He scratched Gus between the ears. "Stay. We'll be right back."

He locked the door and jogged around the rear of the vehicle to meet her. "I would suggest we divide and conquer your list, but I don't want to separate. So we'll just have to hurry. Do you want me to carry Rose?"

"I can manage but thanks." She shifted her daughter onto her hip and lengthened her stride to match his. "Will it be okay for me to turn my phone back on to use my digital wallet to pay for my purchases?"

"It's best if you leave it off. They don't know I'm with you. I'll use my card to pay."

"No need. I have some cash."

"Keep it. You may need it later." He placed a

hand on her lower back and hurried her into the building. "Look, we can settle up later. Okay?"

"Don't guess I have much choice," she mumbled.

"What was that?"

Shame washed over her. He was simply trying to keep her safe. She was grateful for his protection and all he'd done thus far. "Thank you. I *will* pay you back. For *everything*."

A smile split his face. "I know. You strike me as a very determined, independent woman. I just wonder...have you always been that way?"

"No. Not until I was forced to become a single mother."

Maxwell snagged a shopping cart, then reached for Rose and settled her into the child's seat section. "Where to first?"

"We need snacks, a pack of nighttime diapers and a hat for Rose."

She looked around. The layout of the store was like the one where she shopped regularly. Heading toward the grocery section, she made her way to the snack aisle and selected individual applesauce packets, animal shaped crackers and fruit snacks.

Next, she made her way to the back of the store to the children's department. Maxwell trailed behind her with Rose giggling and entertaining him. After selecting the appropriate size of nighttime diapers, Brenda looked through the winter accessories, picking a bright pink knit hat with matching mittens. "That's it. I'm done."

Maxwell guided the cart through the store to the pet section and selected a bag of dog food. As they passed the toy section on their way to the front of the store, Rose squealed and reached for a doll. He plucked it off the shelf, then met Brenda's gaze over Rose's head and mouthed the word *okay*. When she nodded, he handed it to Rose. "This baby looks like she needs somebody to love her. Rose, do you want her? Can she be your buddy?"

"Buddy?" Rose's tiny brow furrowed as she tried to decipher an unfamiliar word.

Maxwell's kindness tugged at Brenda's heart. She did not want her daughter to think she had to have everything she wanted when they went shopping, but a toy this one time wouldn't hurt.

"Buddy means friend," Brenda told her daughter, and kissed the top of her head

"Friend." Rose hugged the doll tightly.

After paying for the items in their cart, the trio returned to the rental vehicle.

"I'll get everything stowed in the trunk while you fasten Rose in her seat." Maxwell pressed the unlock button on the key remote, and there was a short beep indicating the doors unlocked.

Then he pressed the trunk release button, and the lift gate rose in the air.

Brenda removed Rose from the cart, placed the toddler on her hip and turned to open the door. Excited to see them, Gus jumped onto the seat. "Move." She waved her free hand to shoo him away. "Get down."

What was the word Maxwell used to get the animal to sit on the floorboard? Brenda rose to ask Max, but he'd crossed to the cart return. Suddenly, a woman with gray, curly hair darted between the vehicles and snatched Rose's arm. The little girl cried out in pain.

"Let go of my daughter!" Brenda slapped at the woman's hands and twisted her body, desperate to shield Rose. "Max, help!"

Gus growled and flew past Brenda in a furry blur, and then launched himself at the woman and clamped his teeth on the hem of her jacket. Maxwell appeared at Brenda's side, urged her into the back seat with Rose and closed the door. She reached over and pressed the lock button.

"Release," Maxwell commanded, and Gus instantly sat at his feet.

The woman turned to flee, but Maxwell grabbed her by the collar. A young man and woman raced over to them.

"I called 911," the man said.

"We saw everything." The young woman narrowed her eyes and scolded the older woman. "How dare you try to snatch a child! You should be ashamed."

Brenda rocked back and forth, a sobbing Rose pressed to her chest. "It's okay, baby. Mommy's got you. I won't let anyone hurt you."

"My 'k', Mommy." Rose pulled back and looked at Brenda, and a shudder racked her little body. Pulling her new doll to her chest, she wrapped her tiny arms around it and swung back and forth. "It's 'k', Buddy. My's got you."

A police car pulled up, and the people gathered outside the vehicle all started talking at once. Brenda ran her hand over Rose's curly locks, tuning out the discussion taking place outside. "Why don't you get in your car seat, and I'll give you and—what are you going to name your new friend?"

A perplexed look crossed Rose's face. "Her name is Buddy."

"Of course. I'm so sorry, I forgot." She smiled, settled her daughter into the car seat and fastened her snuggly. "I'm going to get out now. You stay put."

"Yes, Mommy." Rose puckered her lips and stuck her thumb into her mouth, her new doll clutched in her hands.

Brenda climbed out of the vehicle and quietly shut the door behind her. Maxwell stood at the back of the vehicle talking to a police officer who was handcuffing the woman, while another officer took statements from the two people who placed the 911 call. Moving to stand beside Maxwell, she placed a hand on his arm. When he turned toward her, she jerked her head toward the back seat. He tipped his head, gave a soft command to Gus and moved around her to open the door she'd just closed. The shepherd jumped inside, and then Maxwell locked the door. With Rose safe and guarded by the dog, Brenda turned her attention back to the woman who had tried to kidnap her daughter.

Brenda had never seen the woman before in her life. Was she working with the men? Or was she part of a human trafficking ring and had simply been looking for a child to grab? Either scenario sent rage coursing through her veins.

Maxwell leaned against the back of the SUV beside her. "They'll need a statement from us, but as soon as they're finished, we'll get out of here."

"Do you think she's working with the men?" Brenda looked around the parking lot for any sign of Jed or Earl.

"I don't know. My gut says yes, but I haven't spotted their vehicle yet." He shrugged. "Of course, the moment she failed at her mission, I'm sure they hightailed it out of here. Which means they will be waiting for us when we leave."

Brenda shivered. He wrapped an arm around her shoulders, and she leaned against him, praying she could pull strength from him.

The officer grasped the handcuffed woman by the elbow and guided her past them. "Folks, let me get her settled in the back seat of my patrol car, and I'll be back for your statements."

"I didn't mean any harm. It was a joke," the gray-haired woman yelled over her shoulder. "He said he'd give me two hundred dollars. That he was pranking his sister."

"Who?" Brenda couldn't resist prodding the woman for information.

The officer glared at her. "We'll get to the bottom of things, ma'am. Let us do our job."

"A bearded man," the woman yelled, and the officer forced her into the back seat of his patrol car. "Six feet tall. Brooding expression—" The officer shut the door, effectively cutting off any more words.

Brenda met Maxwell's eyes. "I think it's time I go home."

"I think it's best we stick to the plan and get you to the Marshals office in Portland. You won't be safe in Fisher's Point."

"No, not Fisher's Point. *Home*. Time to go back to the Appalachian Mountains." *With a stop* in Kentucky to visit Larry in prison. Her brother would be the only one who could tell her what the men were after. Whatever it was, she'd gladly hand it over if it meant keeping Rose safe.

Twenty-five minutes later, after the officers had taken their statements, they pulled out of the big box store's parking lot. The officers had seemed content with Maxwell's story that they had been on vacation and were headed home.

Time to go back to the Appalachian Mountains. The officer had walked over after she'd declared her intent, and Maxwell hadn't had time to point out that the Appalachian Mountains covered parts of fifteen states, including Maine. Of course, there was no point playing dumb. She had to mean North Carolina. But he imagined going back would be a horrendous mistake. Not only because she'd be walking straight into the center of the crime ring her husband and brother had been a part of, but also because, as the old saying went, *you can't go home again.* He'd never really believed it as a young adult, but now he knew better. Sometimes in life, one had to leave home and never look back.

Maxwell cleared his throat. "I'm not sure going back *home* is a good idea."

"Probably not, but I can't keep running from the men after me. Obviously, I'm not very good at hiding or they'd stop finding me." She shifted in her seat, turning toward him.

He frowned, his brows furrowing. How had the men found them at the big box store? There was no way they could have placed a tracking device on a rental vehicle.

"I need to visit Larry and find out what the men are looking for," she declared. "He's the only one who may know why they think I'm a threat to them."

"Larry's your brother, right? Is he in a federal prison?"

"Yes," she whispered, and glanced over her shoulder. "But I shouldn't have any problem seeing him, since my name is on the visitor list."

Maxwell looked in the rearview mirror. Rose was fast asleep, her head tilted slightly and her hand resting on top of Gus's head. Shame rose inside him. He hadn't even given thought to the child overhearing their conversation. Though, even if he had, he wasn't sure that it would have made him stop and pause since he didn't imagine an almost two-year-old would understand much of the conversation. But he couldn't blame Brenda for not wanting Rose to know anything about her father and uncle who'd put hers and her mother's lives in danger.

Maxwell merged onto I-95, headed south toward Portland and the US Marshals Service office. Hopefully, Brenda would understand when he left her and Rose there and headed back to his cabin in the woods in Fisher's Point.

"You said you went into WITSEC when Rose was a week old. Why would your name be on the visitor list?"

"Joe's and Larry's lawyer, Arthur King, added me. Or at least he said he would when he visited me in the hospital the day after Rose was born. Told me he doubted he'd win an acquittal—since Sheriff Dalton saw them bury Ray's body—but he'd try to help them avoid..." She paused and puffed out a slow breath. "The death penalty."

"And was he successful?"

"Yes. They were sentenced to...life..." Her voice broke, and she shifted in her seat and stared out the side window.

Was she thinking about her deceased husband? Maxwell wished he could pull her into his arms and tell her everything would be okay. *Now, where had that thought come from? Push it out of your mind right now. The last thing you need is for her to get the wrong idea. You don't want, or need, a woman in your life. Someone who would pretend to love you until life hit a bump in the road and then they'd show their true feelings.*

"I'm sorry your husband's life was cut short," he said, breaking the silence.

"Yeah, me, too." She still looked away from him. "The sad thing is part of me will always love him. Not just because he was the father of my child but because of the man he once was."

Maxwell wished he could have kept a few happy thoughts in his heart for Ellen. Unfortunately, after she had turned her back on him and told him she'd known he would mess up somewhere along the line, he'd faced the reality that she'd always acted as if she were superior to him. There had been a time, early in their relationship, that his mom had tried to express concern that Ellen talked down to him, but he'd brushed off her concerns, making excuses that Ellen's job as an assistant district attorney caused her a lot of stress, and she hadn't meant the words the way they had come out. "Why is that a sad thing? Isn't it good to have fond memories of him and to not completely despise the man he became?"

"If I could resent him, maybe I wouldn't feel so guilty about my role in the drug trafficking."

Her role? "What? I thought you said you didn't know anything about the drug trafficking that was being run out of your family's garage." Had she been deceiving him all this time? Did she really know who was after her and what they were searching for?

"I didn't." Brenda turned toward him, tears

brimming her eyes and a frown on her face. "But after Joe was arrested, Larry said the only reason they started running drugs was to help pay for the fertility specialist I had to see in order to have Rose. My desire for a child drove my husband to sell drugs, which led to him cheating on me... All of his sins can be traced back to me."

What a horribly selfish thing for her brother to say to her, especially when she was about to give birth. He wanted to tell her she wasn't responsible for anyone else's sins, but how could he? Maxwell had been blamed for the crimes committed by his former partner, and he'd allowed the shame he'd felt for not seeing what Nick had been doing and stopping it before it hurt someone, to drive him away from his family and friends.

A sign announcing the Portland exit in one mile came into view. It was time for a decision. Should he take the exit and drop her and Rose off at the Marshals office, or should he drive her to North Carolina and see this through to the end? He merged into the left lane and accelerated, passing a line of cars and an eighteen-wheeler as he zoomed past the exit he'd planned to take. "So, how far is it to North Carolina?" Reaching over, he squeezed her hand. "I'll drive you to see your brother, if you really think it's what you have to do."

"Really?" she asked—a disbelieving tone to her voice—and placed her free hand on top of his, returning the squeeze.

"Yes, really."

"Okay, but he's not in North Carolina. The federal prison he's in is in Kentucky, north of Knoxville."

"Then, Kentucky it is."

"After you said you didn't know if it was a good idea, I figured you'd take us to the nearest Marshals office and hightail it back home."

"Oh, I seriously considered doing that." He jerked his head to the right. "The exit we passed three miles back would have taken us to a district office."

"What changed your mind?"

"I'm—"

"Mommy! My needs to potty!"

Rose's declaration from the back seat cut off the words he'd been about to say... *I'm not sure*. All he knew was that his instincts were screaming at him to see this to the end.

TEN

"Can you find a place to stop?" Brenda asked, before turning to look over her shoulder. "Try to hold it a little longer. Okay, Sweetie?"

"'k' Mommy." Rose crossed her legs and squirmed in her car seat.

Brenda's heart broke seeing her daughter in distress. She hadn't had a daytime accident in months, not since Brenda had started rewarding her with small prizes for using the *big girl* potty.

Maxwell wove his way through the throng of vehicles to the far-right lane, preparing to exit.

"I'm so sorry," Brenda said, apologizing, heat warming her cheeks.

He must think she was an awful parent for not putting Rose in a diaper on a long car ride, as most parents would a child who hadn't even reached their second birthday. But Rose had always been slightly advanced for her age, hitting milestones. Brenda thought it might have something to do with Rose not being around other children, except for a few hours a week at church services. Good or bad, Brenda had never talked to her child in a babyish voice, always choosing to use proper grammar and complete sentences with her. As a result, Rose was like a miniature adult in a lot of ways.

"I tried to put one of the nighttime diapers on her, but she insisted she couldn't wear it during the day time because she's a *big girl, not a baby*."

"Not a problem. It wouldn't hurt me to fill up the gas tank, and Gus probably needs to *go potty*, too." He smiled at her.

A sign for an exit loomed ahead, and he glanced over his shoulder. "Hang on, Rose, we're almost there."

"'k'," came a soft, tearful reply. "T'ank you, Mash."

Brenda's heart did that same funny flip-flop thing it had earlier when he'd interacted with Rose as they hiked through the woods. She'd spent the past twenty-two months not relying on help from anyone. Now, she wondered what she and Rose were going to do once they parted ways with Maxwell Prescott.

Max sped down the exit ramp and headed for the closest gas station. He pulled to a stop beside a gas pump. Exiting the vehicle, Brenda unfastened Rose from her car seat, while Maxwell began to pump gas. She pulled her daughter into her arms, and Gus climbed over the car seat.

Brenda scratched the dog between the ears. "Stay here, boy. We'll be right back."

"Hurry, Mommy," Rose cried.

Brenda closed the door and did her best interpretation of a speed walker, crossing the parking area and entering the convenience store attached to the gas station. A woman with salt-and-pepper hair and large, black-framed glasses, who worked the cash register, met her eyes as she entered the building.

"Back right corner." She jerked her head, before Brenda could ask, obviously reading the urgency of the situation.

"Thank you!" Clutching Rose tightly, Brenda zigzagged through the throng of people waiting in line at the register and made her way to the back.

A few minutes later, a relieved and happy Rose washed her hands at the restroom sink. "My a big girl, Mommy."

"I, not *my*." Brenda kissed the top of Rose's head then pulled a paper towel from the dispenser and handed it to her so she could dry her little hands. "Yes, you *are* Mommy's big girl."

Rose handed Brenda the used paper towel, and she tossed it into the trash as they exited the restroom.

"Potty prize?" Rose looked around the store, her eyes widening as she spotted a rack of small stuffed animals and shelves full of candy and snacks.

Brenda hated to disappoint Rose, especially since she hadn't had an accident, but she hadn't brought money inside with her. Thankfully, though, she had purchased Rose's favorite animal shaped cookies when they'd stopped at the big box store. Those would have to do as a reward, for now.

"I'll give you a treat in the car." She rushed past the trinkets and treats that were placed at eye level, to ensure children would beg their parents to purchase them, and hurried out the door. A burst of cold air blasted her in the face, causing her to pause a step and catch her breath.

Maxwell was still at the pump. As she watched, he replaced the gas nozzle and waited for the receipt to print. Glancing around, she spotted Gus on the grassy area between the gas station and a fast-food restaurant.

A dark gray SUV with caked mud on the tires and streaked along the bottom quarter of the vehicle screeched to a stop in front of the door, blocking her path. She moved to go around it. The passenger door opened and a short, muscular man, whom she'd never seen before, jumped out and grabbed her upper arm.

"No! Let me go!" she yelled at the top of her lungs. "Max! Help!"

"Mash, help!" Rose echoed and hit at the man's arm.

Maxwell raced in their direction. In the same instant, Gus released a low-rumbling growl and charged toward them, his teeth bared. Before either of them could reach her and Rose, a man dressed in work boots and an orange vest appeared at her side and wedged himself between them and their attacker. The muscular man lost his grip on her arm, and after a quick assessment of the situation, dove into the dark gray SUV.

Earl glared at her from the driver's seat and sped off before the muscular man had his door closed.

The SUV swerved toward Gus, and he darted behind a parked car. And the SUV barreled out of the parking lot.

Maxwell reached Brenda and swept her and Rose into his arms. "Thank You, Lord," he whispered against her ear.

Gus joined them and walked between their legs, pressing up against them. Maxwell pulled back, placing one hand against her head and the other against Rose's, and searched their faces. "Are you both okay?"

"My 'k'." Rose sniffled, plopped her finger in her mouth and laid her head on Brenda's shoulder.

"We're fine." Brenda turned to the construction worker. "Thank you. You saved us."

"I'm glad I could be of help, but I'm sorry they got away," the man replied.

The cashier appeared, a phone in her hands. "I saw everything through the window. Should I call the police?"

"No," Brenda and Maxwell said in unison.

"Thank you." Maxwell shook the construction worker's hand and smiled at the cashier. "I appreciate your help keeping my girls safe. We know who the man is, and the police already know about him. It's best if we get out of here."

He ushered her, Rose and Gus to the rental before anyone could object.

My girls. Why would he call them his girls? Was it only a saying, like *one of the guys*? Or was he getting attached to her and Rose? If it were the latter, she'd have to be sure and let him down easy when this was all over. One thing she was not interested in was having a man in her life. She and Rose had been, and would continue to be, fine on their own.

They quickly loaded up and pulled out of the gas station parking lot. The construction worker and cashier stood on the sidewalk, staring after them.

"Do you think they will call the police?"

Brenda asked. "Will we be charged with leaving the scene of a crime?"

"No, on both accounts," Maxwell reassured her. "What would be the point of calling the police, since the would-be-abductors escaped and the intended abductees didn't stick around? As for being charged with leaving the scene of a crime. There wasn't one. Just an attempt."

"Earl was driving the getaway vehicle, but the man who tried to grab me wasn't Jed. It was someone I've never seen before."

"I'm not surprised it was a different man. Gus really clamped down on Jed's arm in the break-in attempt. Earl probably dropped him off at a hospital to get stitches." Max shook his head. "When I hit Earl, the bullet must have just grazed him, or he would have had to be seen at the hospital, too."

"Could we call the police and have them check the hospitals for Jed? Maybe they could make him talk. Tell us how Earl is tracking us."

"We have no clue which hospital Earl would have taken him to. Besides, there's a good chance he's been treated and released."

"I guess." Brenda glanced over her shoulder. Considering all they'd been through, Rose seemed to be handling things better than she was. Her daughter was jabbering something to

Gus, and the shepherd sat with his ears up, as if he were listening to every word.

"How do they keep finding us?" Brenda whispered as she turned back around and faced forward.

"I don't know," Maxwell replied as he merged onto the interstate. "I didn't see them following us. And I was looking for them."

Dear Lord, how many times can we escape harm when we don't even see the evil coming for us? Please protect Rose. Don't let her suffer because of the sins of her father.

Maxwell scanned the vehicles in his rearview mirror. He'd much rather travel on open back roads so he'd have a clearer view of what surrounded them, but that would add too many hours to their journey south.

"Could they have planted a tracker on this vehicle?" Brenda asked from the passenger seat.

"How? It's a rental." He spared a quick look in her direction before turning his attention back to the road. "There is no way they could have known which vehicle we'd end up in. Even if they had followed us to the rental place—and I think we would have seen them if they had—they couldn't have placed a tracker on it. The rental company kept the vehicles inside a locked ten-foot-tall fenced area."

"Yeah, you're right. We had to wait for the man to drive it out of the fenced lockup before we could take possession. But…" She turned to him excitedly. "What about when we were in the department store? Couldn't they have planted it then?"

"It's possible. But how would they have known which vehicle was ours, unless they had already figured out a way to track us? I knew what kind of vehicle they were driving. I saw it outside the cabin this morning. So I kept an eye out for it as I drove. And I'm sure they were not following us when we exited the interstate…either time." She was clutching at any idea she could, and he didn't blame her. They needed to figure out how the men kept finding them, or there would be no place they could hide.

"If they aren't tracking us through the vehicle, they must be finding us a different way. Could they have put a tracking app on my phone?" She pulled the cell out of her pocket. "I didn't have time to grab it when I was getting Rose out of the house."

He had wondered the same thing, but he'd ruled it out due to all the protections in place on phones these days. "Wouldn't it have been impossible for them to open your phone without a passcode?"

"No. Unfortunately, I didn't think I needed

one. It's just me and Rose, and I keep my phone out of her reach. So, when I purchased the phone, I asked the salesman to disable the passcode and face ID features." She frowned as she scrolled through her phone. "In hindsight, I guess that wasn't too smart on my part."

One thing he'd learned the hard way was that things in the past were always clearer when you looked at them after the fact—through the lens of experience. After all, he'd missed so many signs of Nick taking bribes, putting Maxwell and others in danger.

"Don't berate yourself. You're a mom trying to make things easier any way you can." He nodded at the phone in her hand, never taking his eyes off the road. "Did you find anything?"

"Nope. I went to the app store settings and checked the download history. There's no unauthorized downloads." Brenda sighed. "I don't know whether or not to be relieved."

"Don't give up yet. We're going to figure this out together." *What am I missing, Lord? Guide my steps and help me solve this case without the loss of innocent lives.* The prayer he had prayed every time he hit a roadblock in an investigation came easily to mind. It hit him that in the fifteen years since he'd first taken the oath as a law enforcement officer, this had been the first time he'd tried to do things without fully turning to the Lord for guidance. Remorse settled in the pit of his stomach, making him feel physically ill. When he'd walked away from those who'd let him down in his darkest hour, he'd also turned his back on the Lord. The only one who'd never turned His back on Maxwell.

Forgive me, Lord. I am nothing without You. And I cannot do this alone. I need You by my side to face all of life's challenges. After this is over, and I get back home, I'll try not to be such a hermit. I'll go to church and serve You the way I always should have.

An idea sparked. "Besides you, Rose and your phone, what do we have in this vehicle that came from your house?"

"We left everything at the cabin except the small backpack I use as Rose's bag." She unfastened her seat belt and reached into the back seat area, grasping the backpack and pulling it into the front seat with her.

Unzipping it, she pulled out the contents.

"Put your seat belt back on and then search," Maxwell directed.

"Spoken like a police officer." She tugged the seat belt strap over her shoulder and clicked it into place.

"Sorry. Habit, I guess." He shrugged. "But also, I haven't spent the past sixteen hours trying to keep you alive for you to get injured if we're involved in an accident."

She smiled. "That's a valid point."

Placing contents from the backpack—snacks, clothes and diapers—on the dashboard and in her lap, she searched every pocket, pressing every inch of the pack between her hands. "There's nothing here," she announced, disappointment echoing in her words.

"Well, I'm out of ide—"

"Wait!" Brenda snatched the pack of animal shaped cookies off the dashboard and opened them. Then she twisted in her seat. "Rose, Mommy forgot to give you a treat for going potty. I'm so proud of my big girl."

"T'ank you."

Maxwell watched in the rearview mirror as Rose—her stuffed kangaroo and the doll he'd bought for her clutched in her arms—accepted the bag and shoved an entire cookie in her mouth, chomping happily.

"Let me have Hoppy so you don't get crumbs on her. I'll give her back after you've finished your snack."

"'k', Mommy." Rose held out the stuffed kangaroo.

"Thank you." Brenda clutched the toy to her chest and turned back around in her seat.

"You don't think…?" Maxwell frowned.

"This is Rose's favorite stuffed animal. The one she sleeps with every night. It was in the crib with her when Jed and Earl broke into our house."

"But you left it behind when you ran…?" He guessed correctly.

"Yes. And considering how tattered this stuffed animal is, it wouldn't take a genius to figure out it is beloved. And would most likely remain in our possession if we had to go on the run."

Lord, I hate to think the criminals would tamper with a child's favorite toy, but I pray that if there is a tracking device in this vehicle—and every instinct in my body tells me there is—it's in the stuffed animal and we can dispose of the device. Otherwise, I don't know how we'll stay a step ahead of the men wanting to kill Brenda.

ELEVEN

Holding the stuffed animal firmly in her grasp, Brenda pulled the baby joey out of its pouch and allowed it to dangle freely at the end of the cord attached to the inside of the pouch.

Gripping the stuffed animal firmly in her hands, she felt a hard object inside the kangaroo's belly. Had the men hidden the tracking device in the kangaroo's pouch? With trembling fingers, she dug inside the pouch, grasped the hard round object and pulled it out. She had found the tracking device!

"Well, it looks like Jed and Earl are smarter than I gave them credit for. Hiding a tracking device inside Rose's toy was genius. Too bad they underestimated a momma's instincts," Maxwell said admiringly.

She didn't know if the admiration was for her, for finding the device or for the men and their hiding skills. No matter. The important thing right now was to get rid of the device, and to do so quickly. Brenda lowered her window, and a cold, biting wind whipped inside the vehicle.

"What are you doing?" Maxwell demanded.

What did he think she was doing? "I'm throwing this out of the vehicle so they can't follow us."

"No. Don't. I'll take the next exit. We'll find a trash can outside a fast-food restaurant or gas station and toss it. Then I'll stay on back roads for the next hour and make sure that we're not being followed before we get back on the interstate."

"Okay." Brenda closed her window and shivered. Whether from the burst of cold air she'd exposed them all to or nerves, she wasn't sure. One thing she *was* sure of was that she wouldn't rest easy until the tiny device in her hand was out of the vehicle and far behind them.

Five minutes later, a green road sign listing fast-food restaurants and gas stations at the next exit came into view. She watched as Maxwell checked his rearview mirror and then merged onto the exit ramp. Twisting in her seat, she searched the vehicles behind them but didn't see any sign of the SUV that Earl had been driving earlier.

Maxwell turned into the first gas station, drove up to the pumps, rolled down his window and held out his hand. "Give it to me."

Brenda relinquished her hold on the device and watched as he tossed it into the trash can nestled between the two pumps.

"That's done," he declared as he rolled-up the window. "Now, let's put some miles between us and this gas station."

He pulled out of the parking lot and turned left, speeding past all the other businesses.

"Mommy, my hungry," Rose cried from the back seat. "Chicken nuggets!"

Brenda spotted a sign for a famous fast-food restaurant, of which her daughter was a huge fan. Seeing the sign must've triggered Rose's hunger. She glanced at Maxwell. "Could we...?" she asked cautiously.

"It's too risky. I haven't seen their vehicle, but I'm sure they're right behind us. And they won't waste too much time at the gas station searching for us when they don't see our vehicle. They'll figure out what we've done, then they'll be after us again." He frowned and shook his head. "All we can do is pray they think we got right back on the interstate."

"I understand." She turned to Rose, speaking softly. "I'm sorry, sweetie. We can't stop right now. But Mommy will get you chicken nuggets next time."

"Uncle *Mash* promises to get you something to eat in the next town. Okay, pumpkin?"

Uncle Mash? Why did he come up with that? She hoped it didn't make it harder for Rose to part ways with *Uncle Mash* once they got to a new, safe location.

Rose giggled. "My not a pumpkin. My's a princess."

"Yes, you are. You are a sweetheart princess," Maxwell agreed, then glanced Brenda's way. "You've done a wonderful job as a single parent."

Had she? Hmm. She'd spent so much of her time feeling sorry for herself for the situation she found herself in, she hadn't really thought about what she may have been doing right. "It wasn't a job I wanted. I mean, being her mom is *all* I've ever wanted. Raising her alone, without a father, not so much. However, I'm quickly learning that sometimes in life we're not dealt the hand we think we should be given, but it's okay. As long as we remember God is in control, nothing else matters."

Well, nothing except getting Rose somewhere safe so she could be protected while Brenda went to visit Larry in prison. She couldn't risk taking her to a relative or friend back home. The men after her would surely expect her to do just that. But who could she trust to protect Rose? Would it be too much to ask Maxwell to keep her? He'd been kind to Rose, but Brenda didn't even know if he liked children. And what would happen to her daughter if she didn't return?

Was it okay for life not to end up the way you had planned? Maxwell pondered. For the past year, he'd been convinced it wasn't okay that his life was ruined, and he was perceived—by himself and most of the people he knew—as a failure. But the truth was, in the months since he'd moved to Maine, he had built a successful woodworking business.

Working with his hands had kept his mind busy. Now that he thought about it, he'd been sleeping better at night, too. No longer waking up with a feeling of regret and dread. Sure, he missed being a police officer. The desire to serve and protect was, after all, in his blood, coming from a long line of police officers. But maybe he could start a private investigative service, one where he could pick the cases he accepted while he built his woodworking business. Or perhaps he could open a K9 training facility. After all, he had trained a top-notch police dog when he'd trained Gus. He smiled. Maybe his life was turning out exactly the way it was meant to.

Before he could implement any of these newly formed ideas, he had to get Brenda and Rose to safety. "See if you can find a branch of the car rental company near us. I think it's time we turn this SUV in and get something new to drive."

"Good idea. I hadn't thought about that, but Earl has seen our vehicle." Brenda pulled up a search engine on her phone.

"I found one!" she exclaimed a few minutes later. "It's twenty-three minutes away. Looks like it's on this same road, near the interstate."

"Is there a chicken nuggets restaurant close to there?"

"One point five miles past the rental car agency." Laughter filled her voice.

His heart swelled. It filled him with immense pleasure to bring her a small amount of joy. "Perfect. We'll change cars, and then we'll feed the princess in the back seat. Would you enter the directions on my phone, please?"

"Okay, look this way." She held up his phone, and he quickly glanced at it so the face identification would unlock the device.

"Starting route…" the automated voice announced in a matter of seconds. Maxwell's shoulders instantly relaxed ever so slightly. Although he diligently kept his eyes on the rearview mirror, staying ever alert as he searched for the SUV Earl and his new friend we're driving.

Silence engulfed the inside of the vehicle, and he replayed the events that had unfolded since Brenda showed up on his doorstep.

"I've been trying to figure out how Earl got a replacement accomplice to take Jed's place so quickly." He spoke his thoughts aloud. "Not to mention getting a vehicle in the middle of the night."

"I've been wondering the same thing. What do you think it means?"

"I think it means the drug ring your brother and deceased husband were involved with has far-reaching connections, going way beyond the borders of North Carolina."

"I was afraid you'd say that." She sighed and turned toward him, leaning over the console that divided them.

His hands tightened on the steering wheel, and the hairs on the nape of his neck stood on end. It was obvious she didn't want her daughter to overhear what she had to say.

"If the network is so widespread, there won't be anyplace I can hide," she whispered.

"You can't think like that—"

"No. You don't understand," she said urgently. "I have to face this threat head-on, which is why I have to see Larry. But Rose can't stay with me, otherwise she'll continue to be in danger." Her voice cracked.

The fear in her voice gutted him. He could think of half a dozen reasons separating the mother and child would be a bad idea. However, he could also think of half a dozen reasons it might be the best thing to do. Especially since it would allow Brenda to focus on the task at hand—figuring out who the men were and who was the leader of the drug ring—without being worried about Rose's safety. Only Maxwell didn't really believe Brenda would worry less about her child if she were separated from her. In fact, he was afraid it would have the opposite effect, causing her to make reckless decisions that might put her life, and his, in danger.

"What do you have in mind? If you leave her with someone from your past, it might make her more vulnerable. If the men get to her, they could use her to get to you."

"I know. That's why I think Rose needs to stay with you and Gus. I have some cash. I can purchase a ticket and fly home. Then—"

"That's not happening," he stated.

Brenda flinched and stared at him, wide-eyed. "I'm sorry. I should have realized you wouldn't want to be saddled with a kid, even temporarily. Twenty-four hours ago, you didn't even know who we were. Forget I said anything." Her voice cracked, and she turned to stare out the window. "I'll figure something else out."

"That's not it, at all." *Please, Lord, let her believe me.* Even though they had only just met yesterday, it felt like he'd known her forever.

And, surprisingly, he'd started thinking of her as a friend, and he didn't have many of those at the moment. The last thing he wanted was for her to feel rejected by him the same way his brothers and sisters on the force had rejected him. "Rose is a sweet child. I'd be more than happy to watch her for you. But I can't. Because I need to protect her momma, to ensure she returns to her. Look, maybe we can put our heads together and come up with someone else to watch her. We'll hide her somewhere Earl will never think to look for her. Okay?"

Brenda turned to him, her face streaked with tears. He longed to wipe her face, give her a hug and then whisk her and Rose off to some remote location where no one would ever find them. But that was unrealistic. If the men after Brenda really wanted to find her, they would. They'd already proven they could.

"Your destination is in one mile. On the right," the automated voice on his phone announced.

"We'll figure everything out after we swap vehicles and feed the princess. Okay?"

His question was met with a closed-lipped smile. Not what he'd been looking for, but he'd accept it. Her mind had to be whirling from all she'd been through. There was no doubt she was running through every possible scenario and coming up with less than satisfactory outcomes.

The rental car company was located at the end of a strip mall right next door to a sporting goods store. Maxwell pulled into the parking lot and parked in front of the door, big picture windows offering a clear view of the counter and employees inside.

"I'll go take care of the paperwork. Then I need to run in the sporting goods store and grab some ammo." He pocketed the keys. "Keep the doors locked. If you need me, blow the horn."

She nodded and locked the door as soon as he'd closed it. As he started into the building, his cell phone rang. His dad's name flashed on the screen. Had Tim called Maxwell's parents to tell them of his most recent failure? He closed his eyes, counted to five and opened them again. Pressing the side button, he sent the call to voicemail. He'd talk to his father later. Right now, he had a woman and child depending on him, and he could not let them down.

Maybe he'd ask Brenda to let his parents watch Rose while he took her to see her brother in Kentucky. It wouldn't be that far out of the way to make a side trip to the city. And who better to watch the little girl than a retired police commissioner and a retired teacher?

He paused in his tracks and turned to look at the woman and child in the car. Gus had moved to the driver's seat when Maxwell had gotten out and now sat at full attention, taking in his surroundings. He knew his K9 friend was noting all the vehicles and people in the vicinity, and he would alert Maxwell and Brenda if there were danger.

Opening the door to the car rental place, he strode inside. Time to switch vehicles so they could find a place to catch their breaths and make a plan to outsmart the men after them.

TWELVE

Brenda closed her eyes and bowed her head. "Dear Heavenly Father, I've run all the options through my head, and there is only one person I can think of whom I would trust to raise Rose if anything happens to me. Please, let her be open to the idea of watching Rose. And raising her as her own, if I'm not able to come back to her."

When she opened her eyes, she saw Gus staring at her with his head cocked to the side. Reaching over, she scratched him between the ears, and then ran her hand down his back. "You think I've lost it, right? Well, I haven't. Saying my prayers aloud makes me feel closer to the Lord." In reality, she knew she didn't have to pray aloud. The Lord knew her heart and heard silent prayers, too.

"You know, anyone walking past would think it was just as silly of me to be talking to you." She giggled and took his face in both her hands. Bending, she wrapped her arms around the Australian shepherd and kissed his neck. "Thank you for protecting us. And for keeping Rose calm and preoccupied."

The driver's side door opened, and a burst of cold air rushed into the vehicle. "Hey, what's going on here? Gus, you always get the girls."

The shepherd spun in the seat and barked at his owner.

For the second time in as many minutes, Brenda giggled. "Of course he does. He's so cute."

"That's true. He got the looks, but I got the brains." Maxwell gave a command, and Gus hopped out of the vehicle. "We need to gather our things and be ready to load up when the salesman brings our new ride around."

"You remembered to rent a car seat, right?"

"Of course. I told them I needed a car seat worthy of a princess." He opened the back door and reached in to unlatch Rose.

She watched as her daughter laughed and wrapped her arms around Maxwell's neck, kissing his cheek, the way she often did Brenda when she would bend over to release her from the restraints of the car seat. Brenda's heart melted. Her daughter had always been guarded around men. Except for Grandpa Henry, she rarely interacted with any males, always hiding behind her mother if they tried to speak to her. Maxwell was wrong—he was blessed with brains and looks. Gus was cute, but Maxwell was handsome. If she had met him in a different time or place, maybe they could've been more than temporary acquaintances.

A black SUV, almost twice the size of the one they were currently driving, parked in the space beside them, pulling her from her thoughts.

"That's our ride. Let's load up." Maxwell carried Rose around the back of the SUV and placed her in the car seat that was positioned behind the driver's seat.

He must've asked them to install the car seat there so that she would have an easier time reaching Rose if needed. Brenda grabbed her coat, the blanket and Rose's bag. Then she opened the cargo area and began to gather the bags from the big box store.

"Save some for me." Maxwell appeared beside her. "Go ahead and load up. I've got the rest of this."

Nodding, she followed his instructions. For the thousandth time, she wondered how she would ever repay his kindness.

Five minutes later, they pulled into the parking lot of the fast-food restaurant. "I need to take Rose to the restroom while we're stopped. Will that be okay?"

"That's fine. I'll go inside with you, so you won't be alone if the men show up."

"Thank you." She shook her head. "Those words are not sufficient to express my gratitude." Her voice cracked, and tears stung the backs of her eyes. "You've gone way beyond being neighborly."

"Hey. It's okay." Maxwell parked the vehicle, then reached over and picked up her hand. "You do not have to thank me. I'm just glad I was home and able to help when you came barreling into my house in the middle of the night."

She sniffled and smiled. "It wasn't technically *the middle of the night.*"

"There's that smile." He brushed away a tear that had escaped. "No more tears. We will figure out who's behind this, and you and Rose will be able to live wherever you want, without fear."

For the first time, she noticed the calluses on his hands, just like Joe's. That was the only thing he shared in common with her deceased husband. Having spent a millisecond of time with him compared to the total time she'd known Joe, she'd already realized Maxwell's moral compass was solid and unwavering, unlike Joe's had been.

He leaned close, and her breath caught. Was he going to kiss her? Her heart pounded in her ears, and her cheeks warmed. In all her life, she'd never kissed anyone but Joe—the boy next door whom she'd had a crush on from the time she could toddle around. Five years older than her, he'd allowed Brenda to follow around behind him. Eventually, he'd realized she'd grown up, and he'd decided she was his. She'd never looked at another man. Until now. And it scared her.

"Mommy! My hungry!" Rose's cry was like a splash of ice water.

Brenda pulled back, releasing her breath with a nervous laugh, and Maxwell dropped his hand.

"First, you've got to go potty and wash your hands. Then you get food." She opened her door and walked around to the other side of the vehicle.

Maxwell had already removed Rose from her car seat, but when Brenda drew near, Rose dove into her arms and hugged her tightly.

"Chicken nuggets. Chocolate milk," Rose sang over and over as Brenda carried her across the parking lot.

"I'll place our order while you take her to the restroom." Maxwell held the door open for them to enter the building. "Chicken nuggets and chocolate milk for the princess. But what would you like?"

"I'm fine with anything. Hamburger. Chicken nuggets. Doesn't matter." She made a beeline for the restroom at the back of the dining area.

Thank You, Lord, for Rose's interruption. Please, help me keep my mind clear and focused. You know as well as I do, romance of any kind is the last thing I need in my life right now. Or ever, for that matter. Having Rose is enough. I don't need more.

A large bag of food looped over his arm and a drink carrier in hand, Maxwell leaned against a wall, his eyes never leaving the restroom area. What was taking Brenda and Rose so long? Had one of the goons slipped into the restaurant while Maxwell was placing their food order and abducted them? He looked out the large window that covered half the wall. Gus sat in the back of the SUV staring at him, his tongue hanging out and his tail wagging, obviously excited by the smells wafting from the restaurant. No matter how enticing the scents of hamburgers, chicken nuggets and french fries were, if the men after Brenda were anywhere in the vicinity, Gus would bark nonstop to get Maxwell's attention.

He would give Brenda and Rose two more minutes. If they had not appeared by then, he would go into the restroom and find out what was taking so long. *You can't do that. Not unless you truly suspect Earl or his buddy are in there. Otherwise, you'd only be making a scene. Drawing attention to yourself is the last thing you want to do at the moment.*

Tapping his foot, he checked the time on his watch. Two minutes. Then he'd ask the female manager he'd spoken with earlier while waiting on his food if she'd go in and see if everything was okay. Glancing at his watch every fifteen seconds, he heaved a sigh of relief thirty seconds later when they exited the restroom. Rose toddled beside Brenda, clapping her hands and lifting her knees high with each step despite her mother's firm grasp on her arm.

"I'm sorry that took so long." Brenda was breathless when they reached him. "*Someone* enjoyed the hand dryers a little too much. Since she hasn't had much to laugh about, I let her *play* a little longer. Then, as you can see, she insisted on walking, which also slows us down. But, considering she hasn't really stretched her legs today, I decided not to fight her."

Brenda stooped and lifted Rose into the air, settling her onto her hip. Then she crossed to the door and pushed it open with her back, holding it for him to pass through. "I hope we didn't keep you waiting long."

Maxwell was unaccustomed to a woman holding the door for him, but like her, he needed to learn which battles were worth fighting and which ones were not. So he swallowed his pride. "Not too long. While I was waiting for the food, I asked the manager for a recommendation of a good location for a picnic with my girls."

Brenda stared at him, her mouth agape. Maxwell chuckled. "That's the same look she gave me."

"I imagine so."

"Ah, but I explained I was merely trying to plan a surprise for a little princess, and the weather was of no importance as long as the princess was happy."

"I'm guessing she fell for that line and told you of a nice out of the way place where we could eat in peace." Brenda beamed up at him.

The joy he saw in the eyes that had shed tears earlier sparked a desire in him to stay by her side forever, slaying any dragons that dared to harm her or her little princess.

What was it about this woman and child that tugged at his primal desire to be a protector? It wasn't simply the fact that dangerous men were after them. Maxwell had protected many women and children during his tenure as a police officer. And while he'd always done so to the best of his ability, he'd never felt as fiercely protective as he did in this moment. In that instant, he knew his heart was in trouble. Unless he could capture the men after Brenda, quickly.

Was it time for him to turn to his dad for help? Even though he'd had the idea of asking his parents to watch Rose while he and Brenda traveled south in search of answers, he hadn't truly bought into the idea. The last thing he wanted was for his dad to feel the need to come to his rescue again. Even though his dad had stood by his side during the investigation into the bribery allegations, and had declared his faith in his innocence, Maxwell had sensed the shame he'd felt at having a son who'd been caught up in a situation that marred the family name.

It didn't matter what his dad thought. Or if Maxwell was the family failure, again. He needed help keeping Rose and Brenda safe. Even if it meant letting go of what little pride he had left.

Twenty minutes later, they sat in the vehicle at the edge of a lake, finishing the remnants of their meal. Rose played happily with the toy that had come with her meal, and Gus was outside sniffing the trees and doing his business after eating his dog food.

Time to tell Brenda his plan. "I want—"

"I thought of—"

Maxwell pressed his lips together. "You go first."

"Thank you." She placed her hamburger wrapper and empty french fry container into the takeout bag, then turned to face him. "I thought of someone I can trust to keep Rose safe."

"Oh?" He tried to keep the disappointment

out of his voice. "Is it someone from your hometown?"

"No. It's the nurse who delivered her. Kayla Eldridge."

"I thought you said she was a traveling nurse? Didn't you only meet her when Larry kidnapped her?"

"Yes, but I trust her." Brenda shrugged. "You can really bond in life-or-death situations."

Wasn't that the truth? Maybe that explained the feelings he was experiencing toward Brenda. "Do you even have her number?"

"No, but she and Sheriff Dalton seemed pretty close. I imagine he'll know how to get in touch with her."

"If she's still a traveling nurse, she could be anywhere in the country—or out of it for that matter. You may not even be able to get Rose to her." He shifted in his seat and banged his side against the steering wheel. Swallowing the yelp that wanted to be released, he reached down and pressed the button to scoot the driver's seat back. Then he turned sideways so he could search her face. "I think I have a better solution, if you'll hear me out."

"I'm listening."

"I'd like to call my parents and see if they'd be willing to open their home to you. My dad is a retired police commissioner, and my mom is a retired schoolteacher. Their house has a top-notch security system, and they are great with kids. They have three grandchildren."

"I appreciate that, but I can't leave Rose with strangers."

"Kayla is a stranger to her, too."

"Yes, but I know Kayla. And, while I'm sure your parents are wonderful people, I don't know them."

"I want you to stay at my parents' with her." She opened her mouth to speak, and he rushed on. "I'll go and investigate, see what I can find out. Then I'll meet with the lawyer. If it seems safe, I'll come back and get you and take you to see your brother."

"Not a chance." She pressed her lips together and closed her eyes.

Maxwell waited, not knowing if she was praying or taking the time to figure out what to say next. He hadn't meant to upset her with his suggestion. Though he really thought his plan was better than hers.

A few seconds later, she opened her eyes, took his hands in hers and puffed out a breath. "I appreciate your suggestion. Really, I do. And I realize you want to protect me, as well as Rose, but I have to do this. Seeing Larry and getting answers is my only chance I have of stopping the men after me. I'd like to contact Kayla and see if she can watch Rose. Honestly, I don't think anyone would expect me to leave Rose with Kayla, so she'll be safe there. And if something happens to me—"

"Nothing is going to happen to you. I won't let them hurt you."

Brenda squeezed his hands and smiled, then captured her lower lip between her teeth when it quivered. "*If* something happens to me, I want Kayla to raise Rose. If not for Kayla's selfless act of service, Rose might not be here today."

"I understand. See if you can get in touch with Kayla. If she agrees, we'll take Rose to her. While you try to get in touch with Sheriff Dalton, I'm going to step outside and make a call of my own. Okay?" Tugging one of his hands free, he reached up and tucked a strand of hair behind her ear. Then he caressed her cheek. "I'll be right back."

Reaching into the back seat, he grabbed his coat and stepped out into the freezing afternoon air. He shrugged into the coat, walked over to a bench under the tree where Gus chased a squirrel and sat down. Then he pulled his phone out of his pocket, went to his call history, pressed the name at the top of the list and put the phone to his ear.

The call was answered on the second ring. "Hello."

"Hi, Dad. I need your help…"

Even if Brenda wouldn't let Rose stay with his parents, he knew his dad was the only one who could get the answers he needed before he drove Brenda into the unknown.

THIRTEEN

"Blount County Sheriff's Office. How may I help you?" A female voice recited a standard greeting.

Brenda tightened her grip on the phone pressed to her ear. "May I speak with Sheriff Dalton, please?"

"Who's calling?"

"Tell him it's Brenda Granger." *Please, Lord, let him take my call.*

"What shall I tell him this is concerning?"

"My baby's life," Brenda replied flatly.

"Hold, please."

Her heart beat in tune with the jazz music that came across the line. She closed her eyes and counted, willing her heart rate to slow. *One. Two. Thr—*

"Brenda! A marshal contacted me this morning looking for you," Heath Dalton declared before she could even say a word. "Are you safe? Where are you?"

"We're safe for the moment. But I need your help."

"Tell me where you are. I'll contact the US Marshals Service, and someone will pick you up."

"I don't know." She fidgeted with the hem of her sweatshirt. "WITSEC didn't prevent me from being found by the men Larry and Joe worked for."

"Someone found you? They didn't tell me that. The person who called me..." The sound of movement came across the line and papers rustled. "Marshal Henderson. She only said you and Rose had disappeared and your vehicle was found at the scene of a fire at a rental cabin that you hadn't rented."

Brenda balled her fist and turned to check on Rose. Silent tears flowed down her face at the sight before her. Rose had fallen asleep, her new toy still clutched in her hand and the doll Maxwell had gotten her was her pillow. Tugging the pink throw blanket off the floor, she tossed it across Rose's legs.

"Two men showed up," she whispered into the phone in hushed tones, her eyes never leaving her daughter. "They were searching for something. And they made it clear, once they found it, they would kill me. I barely got me and Rose out of there alive. If it hadn't been for Maxwell, I don't—"

"Who is Maxwell?"

"My neighbor. Only I'd never met him before last night. But at the moment, I trust him more than I do the Marshals."

A sigh sounded across the line. "I don't know, Brenda. I really think you should trust the US Marshals Service. Men break into your house. You go on the run with a neighbor you don't know. Then the cabin you hide in catches fire—I'm guessing that was the men after you, too?"

"It was." She bit her lower lip. He made it sound like her actions from the previous night had been reckless, but he didn't know what she'd been through. Or that her neighbor was trained to protect. "Maxwell is former NYPD. He knows what he's doing."

"Then why hasn't he already transported you to the local Marshals office?"

The driver's side door opened. Maxwell dropped into the driver's seat, quietly closed the door, pointed at the phone to her ear and whispered, "Kayla?"

Brenda shook her head. *Sheriff Dalton*, she mouthed.

"Brenda, are you still there?"

"I am. Look, the reason I called you wasn't so you could lecture me on trusting the US Marshals. I need to get in touch with Kayla Eldridge. I wondered if you had her number and could give it to me?"

"Why do you need to speak to Kayla?"

"That's really between me and her. Do you have her number or not?"

"I do. But her name isn't Eldridge any longer. It's Dalton. We were married ten months ago."

"Oh. I didn't know." This complicated things a bit. Would he prevent Kayla from helping her?

Maxwell frowned. "What's he saying?"

No point keeping him in the dark. "Sheriff Dalton, I'd like to put you on speaker. But, please, keep in mind, Rose is asleep, so we'll have to speak softly."

"I understand," he replied, the volume of his voice softer than normal.

Brenda pulled the phone from her ear and pressed the speaker button. "Sheriff, I'd like to introduce you to Maxwell Prescott. Maxwell, Sheriff Heath Dalton," she said as if they were meeting face-to-face.

"Sheriff—"

"Heath, please," the sheriff interjected. "Now, will one of you please explain to me why you're looking for my wife, Kayla?"

Maxwell raised an eyebrow. Brenda nodded in response to his silent question.

"I wanted to ask her to…take care of… Rose."

"Well, I wasn't expecting that answer," Heath replied.

"It would just be for a little while. I need to go talk to Larry."

"I don't think that's a good idea. You and Rose would be much safer if you'd contact the Marshals and let them move you to a new location."

"Sheriff, did the marshal who contacted you tell you what happened to Marshal Ackerman, the one assigned to Brenda?"

"I've not heard that name, no. I thought Marshal Henderson was the agent assigned to Brenda."

"I've never met Marshal Henderson," Brenda said. "Marshal Ackerman has always been my WITSEC contact. I've tried to call him several times since the break-in but haven't been able to reach him."

"He may be on vacation. Federal agents take vacations, you know," Heath said.

"Maybe. But even if that's the case, I'm not convinced Rose and I are safe in WITSEC. I've been living a very quiet life in a small community, working from home and only interacting with people at church. There's no way I did anything to give away my identity. So how did these men find me?"

"Sheriff, I understand if you don't want your wife to get involved in this. I also told Brenda she needed to let the Marshals Service move her.

But she's an independent woman who can make her own choices. And I support her decision to seek answers." Maxwell squeezed her hand and smiled. "If you and Kayla can't help take care of Rose, we'll make other arrangements."

There was an extended silence on the other end of the line. Brenda braced herself for Heath's reply. She might have to take Maxwell up on his offer of Rose staying with his parents. If they'd be willing to accept the responsibility.

"When will you get here?" Heath asked.

Relief washed over her, and she looked at Maxwell.

"Twenty-four hours," he stated.

"We'll be waiting for you," Heath replied. "I'll text you the address."

Relief swelled inside Brenda. *Thank You, Lord!* Now, all they had to do was drop Rose off in Tennessee with Kayla and Heath, then drive to Kentucky so Brenda could meet with Larry. What would she do if he refused to give her answers? No time to worry about that now. One step at a time. First step, make it to Barton Creek with no more encounters with Earl and his friend. She'd face any other issues when she got to them.

Opening the back door, Maxwell whistled. "Gus, come."

Gus sprinted toward him and jumped into

the back seat, panting heavily. Closing the door, Maxwell slid into the driver's seat and started the vehicle.

"I can drive if you want," Brenda offered. "You must be exhausted."

"I didn't add you as a driver on the rental agreement, but if I get tired, I may take you up on that offer." He circled the picnic area, pulled up to the exit and stopped to check for oncoming traffic. An SUV that looked exactly like the one their pursuer had been driving sped toward them.

"That can't be them!" Brenda gasped.

The passenger side window of the SUV lowered and a hand holding a gun appeared. Maxwell wished he would've taken Brenda up on her offer to drive. Too late, now. Gunning the engine, he floored the gas pedal and zoomed out of the parking area, kicking up gravel behind them.

The man with the gun fired, four times, rapidly. A single bullet hit the back of the rental SUV. Maxwell accelerated, going dangerously fast on unknown roads covered in snow. *Lord, please protect us. I would not drive recklessly in any other situation, but if they catch us, we're dead.*

Gus growled and Rose woke, crying. "Mommy, my scared."

"I know, baby. It'll be okay." Brenda kept watch

out the back. "They're gaining on us. What are we going to do?"

Taking one hand off the wheel, he unsnapped his shoulder holster and palmed his gun. "I'm guessing if your brother taught you how to drive the way you did last night that he also taught you how to shoot."

"Yes. He used to take me hunting when I was younger."

"Ever do any bird hunting?"

"Yeah. I was pretty good at it."

"So you know how to hit a moving target?"

"Yes."

He held out his gun. "You have ten bullets. Don't waste them."

"No, thanks. I'll use the rifle." She climbed between the two front seats. "Once I get the rifle, open the sunroof. I'll shoot from there. I wish the third row had windows that lowered. I'd prefer to be closer to the target, but I'll take what I can get."

"The back window on the liftgate rolls down on this model." Maxwell glanced at the button the car rental salesman had been eager to point out.

"That'll work." She made her way to the very back of the vehicle.

His chest tightened, and he struggled to breathe. He'd never asked a civilian to be the protector. If anything happened to her...

"Slow down. Let him catch up," she commanded.

"What? I don't think that's a good idea. We're trying to lose him, not give him a chance to get off a better shot."

"Trust me. Slow down and let him catch up. Then when I give the signal, floor it."

He did as she requested and reduced his speed. The vehicle behind him shortened the distance between them. Switching his gaze between the road in front of him and his rearview mirror, he watched as Brenda stuck her upper body out the open window. Then he heard three rapid gunshots. Smoke billowed out of the grille of the vehicle behind him.

"Floor, it! Go!" Brenda yelled.

He didn't have to be told twice. He pressed down on the gas, putting distance between them. The car behind them lost control, flipping twice before landing in a ditch.

Brenda made her way back to the front of the vehicle, climbed between the two front seats and plopped into the passenger seat. "Did you see that? I stopped them," she announced excitedly.

"I did. I'm very impressed. I couldn't tell what you hit with your shots, but you did indeed stop them."

"First, I shot the passenger side mirror because the body builder thug was sticking his head out to shoot again. Second, I shot through the grille and hit the radiator, and with the last shot, I took out the driver's side front tire."

"Impressive. We were taught not to shoot at tires on a moving vehicle, that it wasn't as easy as the movies made it look. It seems like the rifle was the better choice of weapon." Though he wouldn't admit it to her, he didn't even know if he would have been able to stop them with three bullets the way she had.

"I agree television makes everything seem easier than it really is. But this was the perfect scenario. It was a moving target, but it was moving toward me, not away from me or parallel to me. So as long as I had the target in my sights, it was doable."

"Beautiful and smart."

"What was that?"

He hadn't realized he'd said that out loud. "Nothing. Good job. Now get your seat belt on and let's figure out where the other tracker is hidden or else they'll just keep coming after us."

She clicked the seat belt in place and then turned to face him. "We've looked everywhere. I don't have any other ideas. There's nothing else in this vehicle that came from my house besides myself and my daughter, and we're not walking around with a tracker planted in us."

He furrowed his brow. She was right. They

had checked everything, including the backpack, which the men couldn't have known she would take with her. And she'd checked the apps on her phone. The phone. He glanced at her phone lying in the cupholder between them.

"Take the protective case off your phone. See if they slipped something inside it."

She snatched the phone and started prying the case loose. "Why didn't I think of that sooner?"

The back popped off, and a slim tracking device fell into her lap. "Found it. This one is different from the first one, less bulky. They must have really come to my house prepared for anything."

"They're drug traffickers. I imagine they slip these devices into their shipments to make sure they reach their destination."

"I suppose so. What do you want me to do with this one?"

He glanced at the map on the vehicle display. It looked like they would cross a lake up ahead. "Throw it into the water when we drive over the lake."

He didn't know how she would feel about a detour into the city. But finding a second device was enough to convince him to make a side trip. He needed rest. And the safest place he knew was his parents' house. Plus, his dad would have equipment to sweep the rest of the items in the vehicle for additional bugs and devices.

Almost exactly twenty-four hours after she had barged into his home, Maxwell escorted Brenda and Rose into his parents' brownstone in Brooklyn. After they found the second tracking device, Maxwell had called his dad and arranged to meet up at a highway rest area an hour outside the city.

Mr. Prescott, who looked like an older version of Maxwell with a few more wrinkles and gray hair, had gone over the vehicle and its contents with a device Maxwell said was designed to find hidden trackers and electronic bugs. Thankfully, there had been no more devices hidden in their belongings. But Mr. Prescott had used his charm to convince Brenda it would be best for them all to spend the night at his house and get on the road again in the morning. Although it really had taken little convincing for her to be persuaded. One look at Maxwell's tired face and a whiny Rose, who'd cried over being placed back into the car seat after she'd been allowed to run around on the grassy area with Gus, had been all it took.

"Oh, my goodness. Get in here and warm up. You all must be freezing." A slender woman, with salt-and-pepper hair and pale blue eyes, greeted them as they walked through the door. She kissed Mr. Prescott and then pulled Maxwell into a tight hug, kissing his cheek. "It's good to see you, son."

"You too, Mom." He pulled back and placed a hand on Brenda's arm. "This is Brenda and her daughter, Rose."

Rose burrowed her face into her mother's neck. Brenda rubbed her back. "She's a little bashful until she gets to know people."

"It's okay, dear. I've raised two children. They both have distinct personalities. This one—" she smiled up at Maxwell "—probably added the most amount of gray hair to my head. Now, take off your coats and come on into the kitchen. I have a big pot of beef stew simmering on the stove, and a fresh loaf of sourdough bread just came out of the oven."

"Come here, princess. Let Mommy get comfortable." Maxwell held out his hands to Rose. She dove into his arms, her eyes never leaving his mother who still stood by his side.

Brenda's heart ached. Without a doubt, her daughter would miss Maxwell once this was all over and they had settled in a new location. *Who are you trying to fool? You will miss him, too.* She pushed that thought from her mind and shrugged out of her down jacket. "It smells wonderful. Thank you for inviting us into your home."

"Of course, dear. Maxwell's friends are welcome here anytime. I'm glad we can offer you a safe place to rest." Mrs. Prescott looped her arm through Brenda's and guided her toward the kitchen. "It sounds like you've had a frightening day. Let's try to make your night restful so you'll be ready to face whatever comes next."

Whatever comes next. Brenda was afraid to even think about what that might be. She was planning to leave her child with a virtual stranger so she could go see the brother she hadn't seen in almost two years. And that made her feel like the worst mom ever.

Plastering a smile on her face, Brenda turned from her hostess to focus on the photos lining the walls of the hallway. There were family photos, ranging from birth to graduation. A photo of Maxwell in his NYPD blues stopped her in her tracks. He seemed so young in the photo. He looked as if he were barely out of his teen years. A photo collage to the left of the picture caught her attention. The photos were snapshots of an older Maxwell—only a few years younger than he was now—and a striking woman with long black hair and green eyes. Their body language and smiles hinted at the love they shared. In the center photo, Maxwell was down on one knee, a ring in his hand, smiling up at the woman who smiled broadly, tears streaming down her face. Questions raced through her brain. Had they married? If so, where was the woman now? Had she died? If they had parted ways, or ended in divorce, his mom wouldn't have left the photos on the wall, would she?

"Go, Mommy!" Rose squealed, pulling her from her thoughts.

She turned and smiled at Rose, who sat atop a frowning Maxwell's shoulders. Brenda's cheeks warmed. He'd caught her looking at photos of him—and the woman, whoever she was. "I'm sorry. I—"

"It's okay." The smile he plastered on his face appeared forced and did not reach his eyes, making it clear his words were simply offered out of politeness and not because it was *okay* for her to get a glimpse into his past.

She suddenly wished she were anywhere but in the middle of the hallway in his parents' home. "Where's the restroom?"

"There's a powder room opposite the stairs in the entry. I'll show you." He turned, and she put a hand on his shoulder, halting him.

"No need." She reached for Rose. "Come on, sweetie, let's go to the restroom and wash up before we eat."

"'k', Mommy."

Maxwell reached up and lifted Rose off his shoulders and settled her feet on the ground.

Grasping Rose's hand, Brenda walked past Maxwell without another word. Why did she feel flustered over being caught looking at photos? *Are you sure you aren't jealous of the woman he'd looked at with such adoration?* That couldn't be it. She hadn't known him long enough to have feelings toward him. And even if she did, she could not, and would not, let the feelings take root.

"Mom, why is this still hanging here?" Maxwell whispered.

"Because I like the pictures and didn't think—"

"Let's move the conversation into the kitchen," Mr. Prescott suggested. "Our guests—"

Brenda guided Rose into the powder room and closed the door, shutting out the rest of the conversation. Would it be wrong to spend the rest of the evening in here? She wished she'd never spotted the pictures. Whoever the beautiful woman in the photos was and whatever her role—past, present, or future—in the family, it was clear Maxwell was not happy the collage had been left on display.

After all he'd done for her, Brenda hated knowing she had created a situation that had caused him pain. If she were honest with herself, she'd have to admit that she desperately wanted to know the story of the beautiful woman.

Knock. Knock. "Everything okay in there?"

"Yes. Tell your mom, we'll be right there." She turned on the water, picked up Rose and helped her wash and dry her hands.

Opening the door, she was startled to see Maxwell leaned against the wall, thinking he'd returned to the kitchen. He straightened and smiled—a genuine, light in the eyes smile—and her heart did a funny little flip-flop.

"I'm sorry. About earlier. I was caught off guard by the photos."

"I gathered as much." She captured Rose's hand. "I didn't mean to draw attention to something you apparently don't want to discuss."

He opened his mouth, as if he were going to say something, then closed it and swept his hand to the side, indicating she should go first. "Let's eat. Then I'll show you to the guest room."

That was that then. End of discussion. Of something that was very much none of her business. They weren't friends. They actually weren't anything to each other, besides protector and protectee. She'd do well to remember that.

FOURTEEN

At 6:00 a.m. the next morning, Brenda sat at the kitchen table drinking coffee with Mrs. Prescott and watching Mr. Prescott and Rose play a game of hide-and-seek in the adjoining family room. Rose hid behind the couch while Maxwell's dad completely ignored her giggling and squirming, making a show of looking in silly places—like a teapot and a potted plant—for Rose, causing her to giggle harder. Brenda could not remember the last time she'd seen her daughter having so much fun.

Maxwell entered the room and paused in the doorway, the same smile from last night on his face. Once again, she wondered what had caused him to leave everything and move to the Maine woods. It was obvious he and his parents were extremely close. *Lord, I pray, whatever caused Maxwell to leave everything he ever knew and move to Maine would be resolved so he could return to a life he so obviously loved. He's one of the good guys and deserves happiness.*

"Okay, time to load up and get on the road, but I don't see the princess." Maxwell winked at Brenda. "Hmm... I thought she might want a piggyback ride, but I guess she's left without us."

Rose squealed and scrambled out from behind the couch. "No, my didn't!"

She ran across the room as fast as her little legs would carry her, her arms outstretched toward Maxwell. Brenda's breath caught in her chest. Her daughter had quickly bonded with Maxwell, and his father.

Brenda had never realized the void not having a father had made, and would continue to make, in her little girl's life. Sure, lots of children were raised by single parents and turned out perfectly fine. She was one of them, her mom having died from complications of pneumonia when Brenda was five. Her dad had done an excellent job raising her and her brother until he passed away in a car accident when she was a senior in high school. Then it had been Larry's job, at age twenty, to run the family auto mechanic garage and keep a roof over their heads. Thankfully, he'd spent his entire life in the garage learning the trade, preferring to be there rather than out playing with friends or doing schoolwork. And Ray Anderson had been there to guide him with the ins-and-outs of the business, having been a trusted employee for more years than Larry had been alive.

An image of Ray and Larry working together under the hood of a car flashed in her mind's eye, and an unbidden tear slid down her cheek. She would never understand how Larry and Joe could have killed the man they'd all referred to as *Uncle* Ray. He may not have been a blood relative, but he'd been family to them. And they'd all three been family to him—the only family he'd had for the last fifteen years of his life.

"Mommy cry," Rose declared.

She glanced up to see Maxwell, with Rose in his arms, standing above her, concern etched in his eyes. Rose leaned over and touched Brenda's cheek. Embarrassment engulfed her.

"I'm fine. Just tired." She quickly brushed the tear away, plastered a smile on her face and stood.

"Of course you are, dear." Maxwell's mom pulled her into a tight hug.

"Thank you for everything Mrs. Prescott." Brenda returned the warm embrace.

"Now, none of that. We told you last night to call us Neva and Hugh," Maxwell's father declared, pulling her into a hug the moment his wife stepped back. "We'll be praying for you," he whispered. "Come back and see us when this is all over."

"I hope to have that opportunity." She stepped out of his embrace and smiled at him.

"You will." Breaking the eye contact, Hugh looked across the room. "Trust Maxwell. He has great instincts."

Brenda followed his gaze. Maxwell, Rose and Neva stood off to the side, exchanging a big group hug. Her daughter had missed much more than a father in her life. She'd also missed out on having real grandparents. Even though Mr. and Mrs. Bauer had stepped in as honorary grandparents to both of them, it wasn't quite the same. If everything was resolved and they could leave the WITSEC program—that was, if they allowed them to remain in it if needed after this—she would reach out to Joe's parents. They had lost a son; they deserved to be in his daughter's life.

"He's never done anything outside the lines and didn't deserve what NYPD put him through. Breaks my heart," Hugh said under his breath, as if he were talking to himself and not her. Then he shook his head, crossed to his son and clapped him on the shoulder. "Take care of these two special ladies, and yourself, son."

Maxwell locked eyes with her over his father's head. "I plan to."

A jolt went through Brenda as if a million-volt lightning strike had coursed through her body. In that instant, she knew Rose would not be the only one who missed Maxwell when this was over and he was no longer a part of their life.

* * *

"I haven't seen anyone following us," Maxwell said as he pulled his mother's midsize sedan into a parking space at the Virginia Welcome Center on I-81. "But it's imperative you stay on high alert, especially while we're out of the vehicle."

"Oh, I will, believe me." Brenda unbuckled her seat belt.

Maxwell exited the vehicle, freed Rose from her car seat and had her sitting on his hip before Brenda rounded the front of the vehicle. "I'll carry her. It will be faster."

"Piggy ride." Rose kicked her feet and lifted her arms.

He tightened his grip on her waist. "Not this time, sweetheart. But I will give you a *piggy ride* before bed tonight."

Rose popped her thumb into her mouth and nodded. Leaving Gus in the vehicle with a promise to return soon, the trio headed up the slightly sloped sidewalk leading to the main building where the restrooms were located. After using the facilities, Maxwell hung out in the lobby near the women's restroom, pretending to peruse the travel brochures.

Soon, Rose raced out of the restroom, squealing when she saw him. "Mash! My washed my hands."

Brenda laughed and scooped her daughter into

her arms. "You mean, *I* not *my*. *I* washed my hands."

"Uh-huh. *Mommy* washed hands." Rose pointed at Brenda's chest before turning her finger back to her own chest. "And *my* washed my hands."

Maxwell laughed, and Brenda glared at him.

"What?" He shrugged. "I think it's cute."

"My is cute?" Rose poked herself in the chest.

"Yes. *My* is." He snickered, plucked her out of her mom's arms then draped his free arm around Brenda's shoulders and guided her toward the exit.

"You have a beautiful family," an elderly woman said as she glided past them.

His chest puffed out at the compliment for the briefest of moments. Then reality smacked him in the face like being doused with a bucket of ice water. Maxwell had let his guard down, and he'd gotten too attached to the spunky woman beside him and her princess daughter. But they were not a family. Never would be. He'd be best served to remember that.

Clearing his throat, he nodded at the woman and stepped out into the noonday sun. They reached the vehicle, which he'd parked near the grassy area designated for owners to walk their dogs.

Opening the back passenger side door, he let

Gus out so he could do his business. "Do you want me to put Rose back into her car seat or let her roam free in the back seat a few minutes while Gus stretches his legs?"

"Let's leave her out of the car seat as long as possible." Brenda moved to stand beside the still-open door. "It was nice of your mom to loan us her vehicle."

"Yeah. Dad thought it would throw the men off our trail. They wouldn't expect us to be driving a red sedan with a New York license plate." He scanned the parking lot. Had they really lost the men after them?

Gus ambled over to them, and Maxwell bent and scratched the K9 between the ears. Ever the professional officer, the shepherd would not spend an excessive amount of time playing when there was a job to be done.

"I'll get Rose fastened." Brenda climbed into the vehicle, her knees on the seat, and situated Rose in the car seat. Then she backed out of the sedan so Gus could enter.

A few minutes later, they were merging onto I-81 South once more. Maxwell glanced at the navigation screen. Six hours and fifty-nine minutes to their destination. "Have you contacted Larry's attorney to have him schedule your visit to the prison?"

"No, I haven't. I didn't realize I need him to schedule it."

"It's a federal prison. They aren't going to simply let you walk in there, even if your name is on the list of approved visitors." He slowed his speed as he neared a section of road construction. "Do you have the attorney's number?"

"Marshal Ackerman gave it to me after Joe was..." She glanced in the back seat and then turned back to him and whispered, "Murdered. Mr. King asked the marshal to have me contact him. Said Joe had left me a message."

"What was the message?" Could it be a clue to the identity of the men?

"I don't know. I never called him. Didn't see the point since Joe was gone and his illegal activity and infidelity had irrevocably broken our marriage. Any message he'd left for me wouldn't change that."

Maxwell reached over and squeezed her hand, never taking his eyes off the road. He wished he had the words to offer comfort.

She patted the hand that covered hers, then pulled free and picked up her phone. "I'll call him now."

"Do you mind putting the phone on speaker so I can listen in?" Normally, he'd never ask someone to do so, instead, he'd let it be their decision. But this involved him, too. Not just because he was driving her and offering protection until they could figure out who was behind the attacks but also because he truly cared about her and Rose. Which frightened him even more than the men after them.

Brenda pulled up the lawyer's contact information, pressed the phone icon, then tapped the audio button and selected the speaker option. Closing her eyes, she puffed out a silent breath. She hadn't seen Larry since the day he'd tricked her into helping him kidnap Kayla, the day Rose had been born. He and Joe had both requested to see her before she entered WITSEC, but she had refused, not wanting to hear excuses, especially after discovering Joe's affairs.

The call was answered on the third ring. "King Law Firm, where we treat all of our clients like royalty. How may I help you?" a female voice said.

What a cheesy slogan! Brenda met Maxwell's gaze and rolled her eyes.

"May I speak with Mr. King, please?"

"Who's calling?"

She balled her fist, digging her nails into her palm as she willed her anxiety to stay at bay. "Mrs. Joe Granger."

"One moment, please."

There was a soft click and instrumental music sounded over the line.

"Mrs. Granger," a male said in a booming voice a few minutes later. "I didn't think you were going to call. I gave my number to Marshal Ackerman months ago."

"Yes." She coughed and cleared her throat. "I'm sorry. I've been…busy."

"That's okay. I understand. How is your little one?" he asked, as if he were familiar with her and Rose.

"Fine—"

"Good. Now, as I told Marshal Ackerman, your husband made me promise to relay a message to you upon his passing."

"Mr. King, I don't mean to sound rude, but I'm not calling about Joe."

"Oh?"

"No. Actually, I need your help."

"Really? What can I do for you, Mrs. Granger?"

"Brenda."

"Excuse me?"

She swallowed and unclenched her fist. "My name is Brenda. I have not been Mrs. Granger for a long time."

"As you wish. How can I help you, Brenda?"

"I'd like you to arrange for me to visit Larry."

"Really?" Mr. King's voice rose.

"Yes. I'm on my way now. I'd like to meet with him in the morning, if possible."

Maxwell picked up her hand and squeezed, offering her strength and moral support. Something he'd been doing a lot of throughout the trip. She returned the squeeze.

Running through the woods into the unknown two nights ago, she'd never dreamed of finding a protector with an equally protective dog to watch over her and Rose. *Thank You, Lord, for putting Maxwell and Gus in our lives. We wouldn't have made it this far without them.*

"Well now, that's rather sudden." There was a rustling sound as if he were moving papers around. "I'll have to call and see if I can get you on the schedule for tomorrow. It normally takes a few days."

"I'd really appreciate it if you can make it happen sooner rather than later."

"Tell me where you'll be staying, and I'll be in touch as soon as I've made arrangements."

"I'll be—"

Maxwell squeezed her hand tightly. When she glanced at him, he shook his head vehemently.

"Um. You can call me at this number when you have it scheduled."

Gus growled and emitted a low, muffled bark. Brenda twisted in her seat, and the phone slipped off her knee, falling between the seat and the console. The shepherd sat on the seat, staring at her, his icy blue eyes sending a chill through her. A shiver ran the length of her spine.

"It's 'k', Gus." Rose stroked Gus, and he laid his head on her lap.

"What was that?" Mr. King asked.

She dug the phone out of the crevice. "It was... nothing. Please, do whatever you can to get me in to see Larry tomorrow. It's urgent that I speak with my brother."

"I'll be in touch." There was a click, and the phone disconnected.

"Well, I'm not sure what I expected, but I guess I'll have to wait and see if he can make this meeting happen." Frowning, she turned and glared at Gus. "And what was wrong with Gus? Why'd he growl at me?"

"I'm sure he wasn't growing at you. Dogs have sensitive ears. He could have heard something in the background of the phone conversation that we didn't detect...a copy machine or some high-pitched noise."

"I guess."

Whatever had upset the Australian shepherd didn't seem to be bothering him now. His head was still on Rose's lap, with his eyes closed, as she sang her favorite cartoon's theme song.

Fatigue settled over Brenda. She faced forward and sank into her seat with her head leaned back. Why had she thought she could barge into a federal prison and demand to see her brother? *Lord, I pray Mr. King can get me on the prison visitation schedule tomorrow. And I pray Larry gives me the answers I need. Otherwise, this could be the most reckless thing I've ever done and could put Rose's life in even more danger.*

"In one-half mile—"

Maxwell twisted down the volume of the navigation system, cutting off the automated voice. He'd follow the arrows on the display map and allow Brenda and Rose to sleep as long as they could. Although he wasn't sure he was doing either of them any favors, as they'd both napped for the past four hours. Which probably meant they'd have difficulty sleeping tonight.

Gus stuck his head between the two front seats and moaned.

"I know, boy. The silence is wearing on my nerves, too," Max whispered. "But we're almost where we're going. We'll wake them when we get there."

The shepherd disappeared into the back, settling onto the floorboard at Rose's feet.

Following the directions displayed on the navigation screen, Maxwell turned onto a private drive and stopped in front of a black iron gate with multiple cameras mounted on its posts. The intercom, encased in a rock column, also had a camera attached. A white fence extended as far as the eye could see, and a long, gravel drive presumably led to a house not visible from the road. He whistled under his breath. Not what he'd expected when Sheriff Dalton sent him the address last night. Heath said that they would stay on Kayla's brother and sister-in-law's property. Sawyer Eldridge was a former FBI agent and his wife, Bridget, managed a security firm in Knoxville. According to Heath, their property would provide the best protection for Brenda and Rose. If the setup at the gate was any indication of the security throughout the property, Maxwell had to agree with Heath's assessment.

Depressing the button on the door armrest, he lowered the window, reached out and pressed the call button.

"May I help you?" an unknown male voice asked.

"Maxwell Prescott and Brenda Granger." Silence on the other end. "Sheriff Dalton is expecting us."

"Follow the drive past the main house and you'll see a red bungalow beside a large white oak tree. Sheriff Dalton is expecting you there." A buzz sounded over the intercom, and the gate opened.

"Have we arrived?" Brenda pushed upright in her seat.

"Seems so." He rolled up the window, pulled through the gate and followed the winding drive.

"I must have fallen asleep." She yawned.

Maxwell smiled. "About four hours ago."

"Really? You should have awakened me." She glanced over her shoulder. "Rose, too?"

"Yep." He nodded. "She went to sleep about thirty minutes after you did."

"What time is it?" Brenda leaned forward and read the time on the display screen. "Seven forty-three. I can't believe I slept so long. And Rose. Oh my, I'm sure she won't sleep tonight."

"I don't know. She might surprise you. After all, it's been an exhausting two days." He pulled to a stop beside a charcoal-gray pickup truck. A man with short, brown hair and a woman with long, blond hair stepped out onto the porch. "Heath and Kayla, I presume."

"Yep. That's them." Brenda smiled and jumped out of the truck, greeting Kayla with a hug.

Maxwell exited the car and greeted Heath with a handshake. "It's nice to meet you. Thank you for helping us out like this."

The sheriff narrowed his eyes and raised an eyebrow. What had Maxwell said to cause that reaction?

"We're glad that we could help. Kayla hasn't stopped talking about Rose since she found out she was going to get to see her again."

The women rounded the back of the car. "Wait until you see Rose. She is so grown," Brenda said as she opened the back door.

Gus bolted out of the back seat, causing Brenda to jump backward with a laugh. Then he made a beeline for the white oak tree. "That's Gus. He's been the sweetest with Rose," Brenda explained as she bent inside and unfastened the car seat restraint.

"Mommy," Rose squealed.

Maxwell grasped the top of the doorframe and pulled the door wider. "Do you want me to—"

"Oh, Brenda, she's a doll baby!" Kayla exclaimed.

"I can bring—"

Heath placed a hand on Maxwell's arm and motioned him to the side.

"Neither one of them is going to hear a word you say until they finish gushing over the child." Heath led the way to a wooden bench near the tree, at the edge of the glow from the porch light. "We'll get whatever luggage y'all have and take it inside after they've had a few minutes to visit."

The women headed inside the red bungalow, Brenda carrying a giggling Rose, with Gus trailing behind.

"So, was your dad able to find out any information about Marshal Ackerman? Do you think there's a leak inside the Marshals Service that compromised Brenda's location? And what's the plan now?" The sheriff peppered Maxwell with questions the instant the door to the bungalow banged closed.

Heath leaned in attentively, and Maxwell knew instantly that the sheriff was an exceptional law enforcement officer. He would protect Rose while Maxwell and Brenda were away.

"I haven't told Brenda yet. I didn't want her upset." Maxwell kept his gaze on the door. He'd hate for Brenda to come outside and overhear what he was about to say. "My dad contacted a friend in the Marshals Service... Marshal Ackerman is dead."

"What happened?"

"He was shot—in his home—the day before the men showed up at Brenda's house. His house was ransacked, indicating he interrupted a burglary." Maxwell pinned Heath with his gaze. "I don't believe in coincidences."

"Me neither." Heath puffed out a silent breath, a cloud of fog the only telltale sign. "And Marshal Henderson?"

"She's a real marshal. Though I can't say I'm pleased with the way she has handled things. She may not have wanted to say anything until they figured out if there was a connection between the murder and the break-in, but the secrecy only compounded the issue."

Heath nodded. "Not knowing who was behind the murder is all the more reason to keep Rose and Brenda under close surveillance. Which, I'm assuming, you didn't think was something the Marshals Service would do."

"Do you?" Maxwell massaged the back of his neck. It was a rhetorical question, and they both knew it. "They may have, but I think their response would have been to move her to a new location and start over. If the men found her once, they could do it again. And I wasn't willing to turn my back on her and the little princess. They needed me."

Heath looked at him with the same expression he'd had on his face earlier. "I'm guessing you needed them, too."

In that instant, Maxwell knew the sheriff had done some digging of his own. Only he hadn't been trying to find the missing marshal. He'd been investigating Max. "Look, I don't know who your source is or what they may have told you about me but—"

"Captain Johnson. Served in the marines with my brother Parker, including a tour of duty in an undisclosed location where Parker saved his life." Heath named Maxwell's former captain.

Max was surprised Captain Johnson would speak about a former employee, as he'd always been a rule follower, but maybe owing his life to the sheriff's brother had made him feel a sense of obligation. "I appreciate you looking out for Brenda and Rose. They've been through more than they deserve and have been let down by people that should have protected them."

"Agreed."

Dread settled in Maxwell's stomach like a stale burrito on a stakeout. "What did he say?"

"On the record, you were charged with taking a bribe and putting innocent lives in danger. After a thorough investigation, all charges were dropped, but you chose to part ways with the department." Heath shrugged. "As they usually are, the details were a little more forthcoming off the record, but I won't get into all that he shared because you lived the experience and know the details all too well. I will tell you he said you were the best officer in the department, and he never once believed you were guilty of the charges. But...he had to follow protocol and couldn't show favoritism, otherwise it would have looked like he was looking the other way because of who your dad is. And that wouldn't have done you any favors."

The reality he hadn't wanted to acknowledge a year ago, when he'd been betrayed by someone he'd thought of as a brother and offended that no one seemed willing to take his side, smacked him in the gut. Looking back now, with the vision that normally came when looking at something after the fact, he realized he would have treated the situation exactly the same as his superiors. He couldn't deal with that right now. First things first, and that meant finding the men after Brenda and stopping them so she and Rose could...what? Move to a new safe location within the WITSEC program? His heart ached at the idea of never seeing them again. *I can spend the rest of my life knowing they are alive and well somewhere in this world, without knowing where they are. Or I can beg Brenda to stay with me, with danger ever present on the doorstep. The reality is no one knows how widespread this drug operation goes. There is no choice. I have to face facts. I will lose them once this is over.*

"Oh, man, you've got it bad." Heath broke into his thoughts.

"Excuse me?"

"If I've translated the myriad of emotions that crossed your face in thirty seconds, I'd say you were shocked at the details your former captain shared. You see things more clearly now concerning that situation and realize you may have acted hastily leaving your job. But if you hadn't left NYPD, you wouldn't have been in the right place, at the right time, to save Brenda and Rose."

"That's all true."

"You're also worried about losing Brenda and Rose once the men after Brenda have been captured."

Shock cursed through him. "How did you know?"

"Because almost two years ago, I was in the same position—minus a child being involved. And I saw the way you watched her earlier." Heath clapped him on the shoulder. "So, let's figure out how we're going to capture the men. Then you can figure out what to do about your feelings."

Maxwell suspected capturing the men might be the easier of the two tasks set before him.

FIFTEEN

"If you don't want to do this, I can turn around right now. We'll go pick up Rose and leave."

"What?" Brenda jerked her head toward Maxwell.

"You've been fidgeting for the past hour. And I don't think it's just because you left Rose with Kayla."

Since the day Rose was born, Brenda had never been away from her. Being in WITSEC, Brenda hadn't had family or friends to leave Rose with for a few hours to go shopping or simply get a break. But that was fine with her. She'd never wanted time away from her child, cherishing every moment with her. And doing her best to safeguard the life she was building. Afraid if she dared to look away, something would happen to Rose and she'd lose her like she had Joe and the life they'd built together. Which, in reality, hadn't been as idyllic as she'd thought it was.

"Leaving Rose was *so-o-o* hard," she replied, her voice quavering.

"I know it was." He picked up her hand, rubbing his thumb over the back of it.

Relishing in the connection and praying she could absorb some of the strength he'd displayed ever since she'd met him, Brenda flipped her hand over and laced her fingers with his. Even though she knew doing so was dangerous to her heart. "I know she's okay. She has Gus with her. *And* Kayla has a fun day planned. She's taking Rose up to the main house to have a playdate with her nephew, Vincent, which will include a trip to the barn to see a young litter of kittens."

"Sounds like fun. Should we turn around and go see the kittens instead of Larry?"

Every fiber of her being was screaming *yes, turn around. Turn around, now.* But she knew she couldn't do that. As much as she hated the thought of seeing her big brother in a prison jumpsuit and facing him for the first time since he waved a gun at her and threatened to kill Kayla in front of her, she knew she had no other choice. "It sounds like fun, but sometimes we have to make the hard choices and do things that aren't fun."

"Well, just remember that I'll be waiting in the parking lot."

"Ahem." Heath cleared his throat. "*We* will be waiting."

Brenda tugged her hand free of Maxwell's and peered over her shoulder. Heat crept up her neck and into her cheeks. Lost in her own worries and concerns, she'd forgotten Heath was back there. He'd barely said a word since they started on the drive two hours earlier.

Dressed in blue jeans and a casual shirt, he'd arrived at the cottage with Kayla that morning and told Max he wanted to ride with them to the prison, in case there was any trouble along the way. Afterward, he wanted to stop by the station and have the sketch artist draw pictures of the men who'd attacked them in Maine.

Brenda frowned. "I'm sorry you have to spend your Saturday like this."

"I'm happy to help. Besides, I've already seen the kittens." He chuckled. Quickly sobering, he leaned forward. "We're about ten minutes from the prison. Neither Maxwell nor I can go in with you since we're not on the approved visitors list, so I want to go over what you should expect. When you go in, they'll have you put your phone and any other belongings into a small locker. You'll keep the key, and after the visit, you'll be able to retrieve your belongings."

"Couldn't I just leave everything in the car?"

"You can leave your phone if you want, but

you'll have to take your identification in with you." Heath tilted his head and narrowed his eyes. "You have your identification with you, don't you?"

She held up the small wristlet wallet she kept in the small backpack with Rose's things. "Right here."

"Good. After you show your ID and lock everything in the locker, you'll walk through a full-body scanner. Then a guard will escort you to a small conference room where you'll wait until they bring Larry to you."

"Okay." She wanted to ask questions about what to expect with Larry. Would he be in handcuffs? Would she be allowed to hug him? Would their meeting be private, or would someone be listening in? But anxiety soared through her like an electrical current, causing her heart to race and her mouth to feel like someone had stuffed it full of cotton balls, making it impossible for her to form complete sentences.

"I know you're hoping he'll give you names—something he's refused to share with the district attorney or investigators. Don't be surprised if he refuses. He'll know that the visit is being video recorded. If he's hiding something he doesn't want a record of, he's not likely to open up."

"Okay, guys, we're here," Maxwell declared.

Brenda turned back around in her seat as

Maxwell drove into the visitors' parking area. He pulled into a space two rows over from the sidewalk, with a clear view of the door, put the vehicle into Park and cut the engine. Then he turned to her.

"You'll be fine." Maxwell pulled her into his strong arms.

She returned the embrace, hanging on a little longer than she should have, as she resisted the urge to beg him to start the car and drive her back to Barton Creek. Brenda puffed out a breath and pulled back. "I know I will."

She shifted so she could see both men. "Thank you for bringing me. For being my bodyguards. I'll be back."

Brenda opened the car door and hurried up the sidewalk and into the federal prison where her brother now lived. The instant she crossed through the doors, a tall white-haired man, sitting in a chair near the entrance stood, his hand outstretched. "Mrs. Granger, I'm Arthur King."

"Oh." Her footsteps faltered, and she accepted the handshake, which wasn't at all like the firm handshakes her daddy had taught Larry were important in the business world. "I didn't realize you would be here, Mr. King."

"I needed to have an attorney-client meeting with your brother, and I've been wanting to meet you. So this was perfect timing." He leaned in, flashed a picture-perfect smile and whispered, conspiratorially, "The proverbial killing two birds with one stone."

Grasping her elbow, he guided her to the check-in area. The next few minutes went exactly as Heath had described, with her showing her ID, locking her wristlet in a locker and following the guard and Mr. King into a tiny room with a small table and two chairs—situated across from each other.

"Mr. King, I would really like to speak to Larry alone. I've not seen him in almost two years. We, uh, have some catching up to do."

"Of course, dear. I'll greet him—let him know I need to speak to him a few minutes after your visit—then I'll wait outside while y'all talk."

"Thank you."

The door opened, and a guard stepped to the side, revealing Larry.

"Brenda! They didn't tell me you were the one here to see me." He rushed toward her, his footsteps faltering when he saw Mr. King. "Oh. I didn't see you there, Arthur."

Larry looked from the attorney to Brenda and back again, his face reddening—starting with his ears and working its way into his cheeks and down his neck. A sure sign he was unhappy about something. "You brought Brenda?"

"No." Mr. King shook his head, his eyes never

leaving Larry. "She came on her own. But I wanted to be here to see this joyous reunion. I know how worried you've been about her and Rose."

Something was off. The lawyer's tone did not match the cordial words. Silence enshrouded the room like a weighted blanket on a fatigued body. Brenda wasn't sure what was going on with the two men, but if her brother's face was any indication, it was clear he didn't really care for the older man. Of course, she didn't suppose prisoners and their lawyers always saw eye-to-eye on things, but she hadn't expected to see such open hostility.

"I called Mr. King. Coming here was *my* idea. I have questions only you can answer." She took a step forward, and Larry took a step back.

"I can't help you." He turned to the guard blocking the doorway. "I'd like to go back to my cell."

"I don't think you want to do that, Larry. See what your sister has to say. Then decide if you can help her or not," Mr. King interjected. He turned to her. "I'll wait outside and give you privacy."

The attorney walked up to Larry and paused, a look passing between them she couldn't decipher. Then he brushed past him and stepped into the hallway. A guard with a beard walked past, looked straight at her and disappeared. She gasped. Earl! Brenda rushed forward, but the guard who had escorted Larry closed the door before she could get a better view. Turning back to the room, she stumbled and fell into her brother.

Grasping her arms to keep her upright, Larry searched her face. "Are you alright? What is it?"

"I thought I saw someone." Closing her eyes, she shook her head to clear her mind. It couldn't have been Earl. "Never mind. I'm sure I was mistaken." The hallway was dimly lit. Her exhausted mind had to be playing tricks on her. Besides, she was in a prison, surrounded by guards. Even if, by some chance, one of them was corrupt, the honest guards would have him outnumbered. And once she made it back to the vehicle, Maxwell and Heath would take over. She'd come too far to give up on her mission.

"It doesn't matter. Right now, I need your help." She clutched his arm, her fingernails digging into his flesh. "Mine and Rose's lives are in danger. And only you can save us."

Larry pried her hands off his arm, crossed to the table and sat down, then motioned for her to sit across from him. "How can I save you? I'm in prison *for murder*. A murder *I* did not commit."

Brenda didn't want to get into who killed Ray.

Whether it was Joe or Larry didn't matter. They had both played a part in his death.

"You may not have pulled the trigger, but you were just as responsible as Joe." She shoved to her feet. "I don't know why I came here. I should have known you wouldn't help me."

"What do you want from me?" he demanded angrily, jumping out of his seat.

"I want to know who is trying to kill me. I wasn't involved in yours and Joe's side business. What could they want from me?"

"That's simple. They don't want the boss's identity revealed."

She gritted her teeth. "But I *don't know* the boss's identity."

"The problem is convincing them of that."

"Who?" Frustration welled inside her as tears stung the backs of her eyes. How could she protect Rose if she didn't know who she was up against?

His eyes dropped to her necklace. "Grandma Alice was a strong woman. You're just like her. You know that, right?"

The door opened and Mr. King entered the room. "Mrs. Granger, I'm afraid time's up. I hope Larry was able to answer your questions."

"I can't answer her questions." Larry glared at his attorney. "But if *you* would get me out of this place, I could protect everyone. I didn't kill Ray! You said I'd be charged with a class B felony for kidnapping and class C for burying a corpse. That I'd be out on parole in two years. Now, do *your* job and get me out."

Mr. King raised an eyebrow. "If I *were* able to get you out, how would you protect them?"

"By keeping my mouth shut. And making sure everyone else does, too. Please," Larry pleaded, grabbing Mr. King's arm. "I want to be the brother I should have always been. And I need you to get me out of here so I can do that. My sister and niece don't deserve to die for the mistakes Joe and I made."

The attorney grasped Larry's thumb, pulled free from his hold and twisted Larry's hand backward. As a grimace of pain flashed across her brother's face, Brenda rushed forward.

"You're going to break his hand!"

The door to the room banged open. The guard rushed to her side, grasped her shoulders and pulled her back.

"No! Let go of me!" She attempted to break free of the guard's hold, but every twist or turn only resulted in him tightening his grip.

"Stand still," the guard ordered in a gruff voice.

She froze, her heart pounding in her ears as she watched Mr. King—still twisting Larry's wrist—walk her brother forward and shove him in a chair. The attorney leaned close and said something she couldn't hear. Then he straightened and turned to her. "Mrs. Granger, it's time to go. I'll escort you out."

The guard released her, and she glared at him. "May I at least hug my brother goodbye?"

"That should be okay, shouldn't it guard?" Mr. King interjected from behind her.

The guard grunted. "I suppose."

She whirled around and barreled into Larry, who was in the process of standing, almost knocking him over.

Despite all he'd done, she still loved him. Regardless of his declaration earlier, until two years ago he *had* been the best big brother. Seeing him being manhandled by his attorney had been a bit much. She would have words with Mr. King on the way out. His behavior was unacceptable.

"I'm glad I came to see you," she declared. "I've missed you."

"Ditto." His arms tightened around her. "Remember, Grandma Alice was an amazing woman, *inside* and out, and the goodness *inside her* that you inherited from her will protect you."

The guard grasped Larry by the upper arm and led him away.

"Come with me." Mr. King placed a hand on her elbow and guided her out of the room.

"I can walk unaided. Thank you." Brenda

tried to pull free, but the elder man tightened his hold.

"I can't risk you taking a wrong turn and getting lost, now, can I?"

"What happened back there?" she demanded. "Do you always manhandle your clients?"

"Only the ones who attempt to show dominance over me." He snickered. "It's important to remind people of their place."

He guided her down a long hall toward a metal door with a window that allowed a small beam of sunlight into the otherwise dark and dank area.

"Wait. This isn't how I came in."

"No. We're taking a different exit."

Panic welled inside her as fear clawed at her chest. Where was he taking her? *Never let them see your fear. It only fuels their desire to get a reaction out of you.* Grandma Alice's words of advice when Brenda had cried over Joe and Larry putting a frog in her lunchbox when she was seven echoed in the recesses of her mind.

She released a slow breath and willed the panic to stay at bay. "Can't we go the other way so I can gather my things from the locker?"

He smirked and increased his pace, almost dragging her behind him. Where was he taking her?

A guard hovered near the door. Would he intervene if she screamed? As they drew close, she took a deep breath. The guard stepped out of the shadows. The scream that begged to be released lodged in her throat, sending her into a fit of coughs.

"Gotcha!" Earl grinned and reached for her arm.

"No!" She looked around, desperate for an escape.

"Get the door," Mr. King ordered.

"No!" Pushing her heels into the floor, she dragged her feet to slow the men down in their effort to abduct her.

"Enough of this." Earl tightened his hold, pulled out a syringe, popped off the top with his teeth and jabbed the needle into her arm.

Brenda gasped. The liquid in the syringe stung as it entered her system, and she felt flushed.

"What have you done?" Mr. King demanded. "I need her alive to tell me where the microchip is located."

Earl spat the syringe top onto the floor and tossed the syringe in the corner. "It's only Versed. Slipped it out of the medical center. Figured we might need it."

Before she realized what was happening, Earl swept her into his arms—one arm under her knees and the other under her shoulders. He held her in a viselike grip, pinning her to his chest. Her brain felt fuzzy and her mouth was dry. She couldn't fight or scream. And there was no one around to save her. *Lord, please, I pray if my time on earth is over that Heath and Kayla will adopt Rose and love her as their own. I also pray Maxwell doesn't blame himself for my death. He did all he could to protect me.*

SIXTEEN

"I really think she should have been out by now," Maxwell declared for the third time in twenty minutes. He almost felt like a kid on a road trip asking, *Are we there yet?* "She's been inside almost an hour and a half. I feel it in my gut. Something is wrong!"

"I think you're right. It's time to check on her." Heath opened his door, then glanced at him. "Well, come on."

Maxwell didn't have to be told twice. He quickly exited the vehicle and met Heath at the crosswalk. They were halfway across when an older model, green, four-door sedan headed toward them, not slowing down. Dashing to the sidewalk, they turned just in time to see the car zoom out of the parking lot and turn left.

"That looked like Arthur King," Heath said.

"Larry's lawyer?"

"He has several clients in this penitentiary." Heath's eyes narrowed. "But I wonder if he was here to see Larry. If he was, maybe that's why Brenda isn't out yet. She may have had to wait until the attorney finished his meeting with Larry before she could see him."

Resisting the urge to run to the front door, Maxwell paced his steps with the sheriff's brisk ones. He prayed nothing had happened to Brenda. Surely she was safe inside the walls of the prison with all the guards. Earl or one of his buddies wouldn't have been able to get past security...would they?

When they reached the entrance, Heath put a hand out to open the door and turned toward him. "I'll take the lead."

As much as Maxwell wanted to go into the building and demand answers, he knew that tactic would not be beneficial. "Of course. You're the local law enforcement officer." *I'm just a civilian.*

Heath led the way, walking up to the female officer sitting at the check-in desk and peering at her name tag. "Good morning, Officer Mabrey. I'm Sheriff Dalton, from Blount County." He presented his ID and motioned for Maxwell to do the same. "Mr. Prescott and I drove the sister of one of your prisoners here this morning to visit with him. The visitation should have been over by now, but we've not seen her come out."

The officer examined both IDs. Then she

placed them on a scanner, scanning them into her computer before returning them. "What is the name of the visitor, and who was she visiting?"

"Brenda Granger. She is visiting Larry Frye."

She clicked a few keys on her keyboard. "She checked in at 9:15. But she hasn't signed out yet."

"Would it be possible to find out how much longer she will be? We really need to get back to Barton Creek, or I wouldn't ask." He smiled and leaned his arm on the counter. "You know how it goes. Try to do a good deed, and... Some people take advantage."

"Oh, I know only too well." She nodded toward the row of chairs. "If you'll have a seat, I'll have someone notify Mrs. Granger that you need her to hurry."

"Thank you, Officer Mabrey."

Heath pointed at vacant seats away from the handful of people waiting to see friends and loved ones who lived behind the bars of the prison. Crossing to the hard, plastic chairs, Maxwell sat in the one closest to the window, and Heath dropped into the one next to him. Maxwell would have rather paced, but doing so would have brought unnecessary attention to them.

"You handled that well." Maxwell watched as Officer Mabrey spoke on the phone, casting glances in their direction. "How'd you know she'd fall for the *tried to do a good deed but was taken advantage of* scenario?"

"I didn't." Heath shrugged. "There are givers and takers in this world. And I believe many people have experienced giving someone a helping hand only to have them want more and more from them, so I took a chance that she could relate."

"It worked. Hopefully, Brenda and Larry's meeting is almost over, and she'll walk through that locked metal door any minute now."

"Maybe."

"Sheriff Dalton," Officer Mabrey called, fifteen minutes later. "Please come to the desk."

Maxwell and Heath were on their feet before she had finished her sentence. All eyes in the room were on them as they hurried to the desk. A tall man dressed in professional attire had joined Officer Mabrey at the desk. When they drew near, he motioned them to the side.

"I'm Warden Rutter. Follow me, please." Without waiting for a reply, he led them down a series of halls to his office.

Once they were inside, he closed the door and motioned for them to sit in the chairs in front of his desk, then he settled into the chair behind the desk.

"What is going on, Warden Rutter?" Heath asked.

"Where is Brenda Granger?" Maxwell's patience had worn thin, and he needed immediate answers.

"Inmate Frye's attorney arranged a meeting with him today, at the same time as Mrs. Granger's."

"Arthur King. We saw him leaving the parking lot. He seemed in a rush—" Heath turned to Maxwell, wide-eyed.

Maxwell gasped. "Like he was running from something...or had stolen something." He pushed to his feet, planted both hands on the warden's desk and leaned forward. "Brenda's life is in danger. We have got to find her. Now!"

"I've already notified the local sheriff's office. They've issued an APB for Arthur King's vehicle," the warden replied.

Heath stood and placed a hand on Maxwell's shoulder. "What are you not telling us?"

Warden Rutter sighed. "When Officer Mabrey called Officer Brown—the officer assigned to escort Frye to and from his cell—to ask him to end the meeting and send Mrs. Granger to the visitor's waiting area, he told her the meeting ended twenty minutes ago. He said Mr. King and Frye had exchanged words and Frye had put his hands on his attorney. Officer Brown had to restrain Mrs. Granger to keep her from getting in the middle of the scuffle. Once the skirmish was over, he escorted the inmate back to his cell, and Mr. King volunteered to escort Mrs. Granger *out*."

"Out. Where?" Maxwell asked through gritted teeth.

"Mr. Prescott, I understand your concern. And I want to get to the bottom of this as quickly as you do. One of my officers was seen on camera interacting with Mr. King and Mrs. Granger. Then my officer carried Mrs. Granger outside and placed her in Mr. King's vehicle."

"Carried? Why would Brenda need to be carried out?"

"I've asked the officer to join us. I assure you, we will get an expl—"

There was a knock, and the office door opened. "I was told you wanted to see me, Warden."

At the sound of the voice he'd first heard in his yard three nights ago, Maxwell whirled around, locking gazes with Earl.

"I'll come back." Earl turned to leave, but an officer who looked like a linebacker blocked his path. Earl tried to push past the guard, but the muscular officer folded his arms and stood his ground.

"That man needs to be arrested for attempted murder and arson!" Maxwell demanded, taking a step toward the man who'd tormented Brenda, trying to kill her.

The warden stood, blocking Max's path, looking from him to Earl and back again. "Attempted murder and arson?"

"Yes, sir. He showed up in Maine, where Mrs. Granger was living in witness protection, and attempted to kill her and her daughter. Multiple times." Maxwell narrowed his eyes, taking in Earl's stance. "Check his left shoulder. I hit him with a bullet during one of the attacks. He has to have a wound."

Earl smirked and folded his arms.

Realization dawned on Maxwell. "You were wearing a bulletproof vest." No wonder the bullet hadn't stopped him. "No matter. There will still be a nasty bruise."

"Officer Zimmerman, explain yourself," the warden ordered.

"I'd like to call my lawyer," Earl replied.

"Of course, you have every right to call your lawyer. But I'd advise you to tell us where Mr. King took Mrs. Granger and what was in the syringe that you injected into her."

He'd drugged Brenda? Maxwell balled his fist and took a step around the warden, but Heath put a restraining hand on his arm.

"It won't help the situation," Heath advised.

"Might not, but it sure would make me feel

better in the moment." Maxwell clenched his teeth.

"Listen to your friend," Earl said with a smirk. "Besides, you can't protect her now. And *I will not tell* you anything."

The warden motioned to the other guard. "Put him in handcuffs and place him in a holding cell until the local authorities arrive to take him. Stand guard and do not let him make a phone call. Can't have him warn Arthur King we're on to him."

"No. Wait! You have to force him to tell us where King took Brenda," Maxwell demanded, as Earl was being handcuffed.

Earl locked eyes with him, laughing as the other guard dragged him away.

"Warden Rutter, I appreciate you have to do things according to protocol." Maxwell turned to the one person in the room who could still help them get answers, knowing the prison had strict rules on inmate visitations. "Believe me, I do, but could we please talk to Larry Frye? If Arthur King is the head of the drug ring Larry was working for, he might have an idea where the attorney would have taken Brenda."

Maxwell's throat tightened. He'd always been a strictly by-the-book rule follower, which was why it had hurt so much when the people in his life had thought he'd done something illegal.

And he'd never thought he would be the one to ask another law enforcement officer to bend the rules, but he could not let his sense of right and wrong cost him the woman he loved. She and her little princess had wormed their ways into his heart, and for the first time in a long time, he felt all the emotions that went with caring for someone other than himself. He would not give up until he'd found Brenda, told her he loved her and taken her home to Rose.

Brenda moaned. Who was operating the jackhammer inside her head, and how could she make them stop?

"Good. You're waking up. I hope you've enjoyed your nap," a male voice declared sarcastically. "Though I must say you slept longer than Earl said you would."

She bolted upright and instantly regretted it, clutching her head. "Ow!"

"Aw. Does your head hurt?"

Brenda peered in the direction the voice had come from. Arthur King stepped out of the shadows, a gun in his hand trained on her. Carefully turning her head, she took in her surroundings. She was sitting on the floor of a living room in an old single-wide mobile home. The shaggy, brown carpet was stained with what she could only hope was not urine, though it smelled foul, and graffiti had been spray painted on all the walls, from floor to ceiling. On the opposite end of the room was a kitchen with faded floral wallpaper, grimy cabinets and torn, green linoleum. There was no furniture in the trailer as far as she could see, but a pillow and a patchwork blanket lay crumpled in one corner, making her wonder if someone, maybe the graffiti artist, slept here occasionally.

She sat up straighter and pressed her back against the wall, pulling her knees to her chest and hugging them close. Surprisingly, he hadn't tied her up. But then again, he had a weapon and she didn't, so why bother? "Where are we?"

"My childhood home." He looked around. "Who would have thought that someone who grew up in this dump could have turned out so well, become a successful lawyer and all?"

A rat ran across the kitchen floor. Brenda jumped, biting back a scream, and her hand connected with one of the dark, wet spots on the floor. Bile burned the back of her throat. *Don't be sick.* Forcing herself to swallow, she wiped the hand on her jeans and Arthur King laughed manically. She was in the presence of someone who was sheer evil. A shiver racked her body.

Recalling a sermon her preacher had given a few weeks earlier about not fearing what man could do to the earthly body, she straightened her spine and shuttered her face. *Stay composed. Don't let him incite a reaction.* This was not the first time she had been in a difficult situation. She would not allow herself to fall apart.

Dear Lord, I want to live to see Rose as a grown woman with her own children one day. But if I was only meant to be with her for a little while, and it is time for me to go to my heavenly home, I pray Rose will remember me and that she will grow up knowing how much I loved her.

"What do you want from me?" Resolve welled inside her. She would get answers before she died. "As you very well know, Joe and Larry kept me in the dark concerning their side business. I didn't even know you were the person running the drug ring, so why would you fear me so much that you'd kill me and take me away from my innocent daughter?"

"I want the microchip." He strode toward her.

She resisted the urge to flinch as he drew near. "What microchip?" Brenda locked eyes with him. "When the men broke into my house, I overheard them saying they had to find the microchip. But I didn't know what they were talking about, and I still don't. Because I'm not hiding a microchip."

Pressing her back to the wall, she pushed herself upward until she was standing. She would not cower in fear.

Before she could react, the lawyer grabbed her by the shoulders. The gun, still in his right hand, pressed painfully against her left shoulder.

"Joe said you had it. Tell me where it is," he demanded, shaking her—the back of her head repeatedly banging against the wall.

"I... Don't... Have it! Stop shaking me!" She jerked sideways, catching him off guard and causing the gun to slip from his hand.

Instinctively, she dove to the ground and reached for the weapon. Inches from her goal, he stepped on her hand, and she yelped in pain.

"You mustn't be naughty." He ground the toe of his shoe against her fingers, as if he were putting out a cigarette butt, and there was a loud pop.

She closed her eyes and bit her lip, refusing to allow him any more pleasure. He lifted his foot and kicked her in the side.

"Don't pull another stunt like that, or I will shoot you instantly."

She opened her eyes. He stood a few feet away, the weapon trained on her. Brenda crawled backward, silently wincing, until she was seated against the wall once more. The metallic taste of blood filled her mouth. If she swallowed it, she would vomit. She glanced around. What was one more stain when the carpet was as nasty as what she was sitting on? She spat on the floor, then wiped her mouth with the back of her hand.

"Gross! Didn't your mother teach you any manners? Maybe Rose would be better off without you."

Her mom had taught her not to cower to bullies, to call their bluff and beat them at their own game. "You're probably right. After all, what kind of motherly example can I be? I picked a man who was a liar and a cheat to be my husband and the father of my child."

How different would her life have been if she'd picked a different man to fall in love with? She couldn't even entertain that thought. If she wouldn't have married Joe, she wouldn't have Rose, and she could not imagine a world without Rose in it.

"Back to the topic of Joe. I'm not playing games. I want the microchip he gave you with details of the organization."

"If I had something like that, wouldn't I have turned it over to the police?"

"Uh-uh." Arthur shook his head. "He said it was an insurance policy to keep you and him and your child safe. And you wouldn't turn it over as long as you were left alone."

"Then why didn't you leave me alone?"

He frowned. "The longer you spent in witness protection, creating a new life, the greater the risk you'd decide holding on to it wasn't worth it. Especially if you fell in love with someone else."

An image of Maxwell flashed in her mind. She *had* fallen in love with someone else. And she did not want to leave this life before she told him how she felt. She'd had too many regrets—with thoughts of what she should've or could've done differently—she didn't want to add another regret to the list. If there was the slightest chance Maxwell loved her, too, she had to know. Brenda could picture him playing with Rose, maybe having a tea party, while she cooked dinner.

As she often did when she was in deep thought, she reached up to grasp her Grandma Alice's broach and froze in mid-action. She knew where the microchip was hidden. She brought her hand to her mouth, bent at the waist and coughed repeatedly. With her hair acting as a shield, she tucked her necklace into her shirt, then straightened.

Using her uninjured hand, and the wall for support, she stood once again, facing him with pretend bravo. "I don't have the microchip, but if you promise to let me live, I will help you find it."

"Keep talking, and I will consider it after I hear what you have to say."

Lord, I know he doesn't plan to let me live,

but please, give me the words to keep him talking until Maxwell and Heath have time to find me. Because I know they are searching, and I don't want to die. Not when Rose and I have a chance at a happily-ever-after ending.

SEVENTEEN

Maxwell peered through the binoculars Heath had insisted they stop at a sporting goods store to purchase, after Larry told them about the mobile home near Rocky Top, Tennessee, where Arthur King held clandestine meetings. Maxwell had tried to convince Heath stopping would take too long and could prevent them from reaching Brenda in time. But the sheriff had stood his ground, telling Maxwell taking a few minutes to gather what they needed would serve them better in the long run than barging in unprepared.

Thanks to the binoculars—and the windows in the mobile home, which either didn't have blinds covering them or had blinds that were broken and dangling, leaving gaps he could see through—he could assess the situation. From his hiding spot behind a rusty metal shed, fifty yards from the old, run-down mobile home where Arthur King held Brenda hostage, Maxwell had a clear view inside of everything taking place in the trailer. As he took in the scene before him, Max had to admit that Heath had been right.

"I know you told the sheriff we would wait for him. But if he doesn't arrive soon, I'm going in without him." He lowered the binoculars and held them out to Heath. "There's a bruise on her face. It looks like he has beaten her."

Heath accepted the binoculars. "I don't see anyone else inside with them. Did you?"

"No. Just him and Brenda."

"I don't know what she's telling him, but she has his full attention." Heath handed the binoculars back to Max. "I know your first instinct is to rush the scene, guns blazing and get her out of there, but you know as well as I do, doing some Hollywood movie stunt like that could cost her, her life."

"This isn't Brenda's first time being involved in a hostage situation. Trust her to do what she has to do to stay alive." Heath lifted his long-range rifle to his shoulder and looked through the scope. "If there seems to be any movement inside that shows her life is in imminent danger, we'll both go in."

"She told me Larry used her as bait to abduct Kayla," Maxwell commented, once again putting the binoculars to his eyes. "You rescued her then. I know we'll do it this time, too."

He could not allow any room for doubt to enter his mind. If he did, and fear took over, he was afraid he'd make a mistake that cost Brenda her life. And he would not be able to live with himself if that were to happen.

"As much as I would love to take credit for that rescue, Kayla is the one that saved them. She outsmarted Larry as we were getting ready to storm the residence. Then I came in and assisted with Rose's birth."

Maxwell glanced at Heath. He hadn't known about the sheriff assisting with the birth. Once this was over, he would owe the man beside him a debt of gratitude for saving the lives of the two people who had entered his world in a flash and whom he loved more than life itself.

"I don't care who saves her. Whether Brenda does it herself or if you or I put a bullet through his head. The important thing is getting her out alive so she can come home to Rose and me."

"We will make that happen. Because she deserves to know how you feel. And she deserves a life free from looking behind her for monsters in the shadows."

If Brenda would allow it, Maxwell would spend the rest of his life making sure she knew she was loved and protected. The irony wasn't lost on him that he'd known Ellen four months before he declared his feelings and four years before he proposed, but he had only known Brenda four days and he couldn't imagine his life without her in it. If he failed to save her, he would never recover from the pain that would follow. The faint sound of a vehicle drew his attention, and he swept the binoculars in the direction it came from. "Looks like reinforcements have arrived. Two sheriffs' vehicles just parked up the road."

Heath's phone buzzed. Sliding his finger across the screen, he answered the phone and lifted it to his ear. "Sheriff Dalton... Yes... We have eyes on the suspect. He and Mrs. Granger are in the living room. He has a weapon... Sounds good."

Heath disconnected the call and shoved his phone into his back pocket. "That was Sheriff Thorne. He and two of his deputies have arrived. They're going to get as close as they can while staying out of sight. However, they'll wait for my signal to move in, since we've already evaluated the situation."

Relief washed over Maxwell. He had dreaded the sheriff showing up on scene and taking over. "I'm surprised, considering we're in his district."

Heath shrugged. "I would do the same if the situation were reversed. We don't posture around here. This is a team effort."

Maxwell couldn't help but wonder what it

would be like to work where people from different departments or districts didn't try to always take charge or receive the most recognition. A place where they believed the best in each other and didn't jump to conclusions. Maybe instead of giving up on a career in law enforcement, which he had loved, he needed to consider a relocation. But those decisions could wait until Brenda was in his arms, because nothing was more important than her.

As he watched through the binoculars, King grabbed Brenda and pulled her toward the front door, his gun pointed at her side. "He's bringing her out the front. I'll take the left side. You take the right."

Max raced to the left side of the trailer, not waiting for Heath's response or caring that he'd just taken the lead on this mission. He hoped the sheriff's ideology of not posturing and it being a team effort extended to him, too. But if not, he didn't care. The only thing that mattered was getting Brenda away from the killer who had her in his grasp.

"Can you loosen your grip a little? It's not like I'm going to run. If I did, you'd shoot me in the back, and I can't let my daughter think I died a coward."

Arthur chuckled. "I like your spunk. I could

use someone like you in my organization. Too bad I didn't approach you with my business offer instead of Joe."

"I would have refused you flat out."

"You might not have. After all, money talks."

"I'm not interested in *dirty* money. My treasures are laid up in heaven."

He guided her down the wobbly steps someone had made from stacked eight-inch concrete blocks that were topped with cracked and crumbly four-inch concrete cap blocks—none of it cemented in place. For a brief second, she wondered how he got her inside without dropping her and breaking her neck.

"Your loss. You and your daughter could have lived in a mansion and never worried about a thing. Too bad she has to be an orphan now."

Brenda's breath caught, and she stumbled on the next to the last step. She'd never once doubted that he intended to kill her, but hearing him so blatantly stating his intention was unnerving.

"Watch it!" His fingers bit into her upper arm as he jerked her upright.

Intent upon reminding him of his promise never to approach Rose, she spun to face him. A piece of the cap block slid and sent her into a backward free fall.

Instinctively, she grasped his arm to break her

fall and pulled him down with her. They landed with a thud. A piercing pain shot through her, and she couldn't breathe.

"You clumsy idiot!"

As if in slow motion, she watched as Arthur scrambled off her, grabbed his gun, which had landed a few feet away, rose and pointed it at her head. She closed her eyes. "Lord, please, make it quick. Don't make me suffer," she whispered.

"Drop the gun!" Heath Dalton ordered from somewhere nearby.

Arthur looked over his shoulder. Using her forearms and heels, she crawled backward, scrambling to put as much distance between her and him as possible. He turned his attention back to her, smiled the evilest smile she'd ever seen and raised the barrel of the gun once more. "I'll see you in—"

Gunshots rang out, and a guttural scream ripped from her throat as she watched multiple bullets hit Arthur in his upper body. He fell to the ground, and police officers swarmed in.

Strong arms wrapped around Brenda and cradled her as she sobbed.

"Shhh. It's okay. I've got you," Maxwell whispered in her ear.

She buried her face in his chest and put her arms around him. Pain radiated through her body. "Ow."

Maxwell pulled back, swept her hair out of her face and kissed her forehead. "Where does it hurt?"

She closed her eyes and puffed out a breath, desperate to push the pain away. "Everywhere. I'm pretty sure I have at least two broken fingers on my right hand and some cracked ribs."

"Someone, call an ambulance!" Maxwell ordered.

"They're already on their way." Heath knelt beside them. "Are you in much pain?"

"Only when I breathe... So, yeah, a lot of pain." She looked over at Arthur King's motionless body. "Is he dead?"

"I'm afraid so. But he knew what would happen before he pointed the gun at you with police officers surrounding him." Heath placed a hand on her shoulder. "We'll never know why he chose that over surrendering. But, thanks to Larry, we now have the names of some of his other associates, and we can start shutting down their drug operation."

"Wait!" Brenda lifted her hair off her neck with her left hand. "Help me get my necklace off."

Maxwell unclasped the necklace and dropped it into her hand. She held it out to Heath.

"This was my grandmother's broach. Joe had it made into a necklace for me. I think you'll find the microchip Arthur King was searching for hidden inside it."

Heath examined the necklace. "There's a tiny groove. Hang on." He turned toward the group of officers hovering near the body. "Sheriff Thorne, do you have a pocketknife?"

"Sure do." A tall, middle-aged man with a crew cut walked over and handed Heath a small knife. "What do you have there?"

"If Mrs. Granger's hunch is right, it's evidence." Heath pried the back off the broach, and a tiny black-and-silver object fell out.

He held it up and whistled. "If Arthur King thought this was worth dying for, I would imagine this small device contains enough information to take a lot of drugs and dealers off the streets."

She shuddered. Maxwell slid his arms out of his jacket and tucked it around her.

An ambulance siren pierced the air. Maxwell dug into one of the jacket pockets and extracted his keys, tossing them to Heath. "I'll go with Brenda. Can you swing by the hospital when you're finished up here?"

"Of course." He clapped Max on the shoulder and stood. "After I turn the microchip over to the FBI."

Brenda wanted to insist she didn't need anyone to ride in the ambulance with her, but it would have been a lie. She needed Max by her side, now and always. "Thank you."

"For what, sweetheart?"

"For one, calling me sweetheart. I like it. But mainly for staying with me. I know I should be strong, but I can't." Her voice cracked, and a tear slid down her cheek.

He brushed the tear away. "You are the strongest woman I've ever met. I did not know what I was missing in life until you and Rose barreled into my house. I know I shouldn't be thankful for all that you've been through, but in a way I am. Because that's what brought you to me."

Her heart swelled. "I love you, Maxwell."

"I love you, too, sweetheart." He claimed her lips in the sweetest, most tender kiss she'd ever experienced.

"Sir, we need you to move back." A female medic brushed past Maxwell, pushing her way between them so she could examine Brenda.

Maxwell shifted his position so he could hold her hand while giving the medic room to work. His steadying presence soothed her anxiety, and she knew, from that moment on, with him by her side, she could handle all of life's ups and downs.

EPILOGUE

With all eyes on him, Maxwell resisted the urge to fidget as he stood in his black suit at the front of the chapel decorated with pink and white roses, looking out over the small congregation of people he and Brenda had invited to share in their day—the day they officially became a family.

The minister clapped him on the back. "Are you ready?"

"Yes, sir." Maxwell smiled, his heart swelling with love and gratitude. "I've been ready for this day ever since Brenda and Rose barged into my life four months ago."

The music began, and the doors at the back of the chapel opened. His father escorted his mother down the aisle. Maxwell stepped forward, gave his mother a kiss and hug, then shook his father's hand, pulling him into a warm embrace. He'd never truly understood his parents' unconditional love and the depths they would go to for their children until Rose had come into his life. She might not be his biological child, but she was his daughter. And he had the legal paperwork to prove it, having signed the adoption papers the day before. He would spend the rest of his life protecting her, encouraging her and cheering her on.

He watched as his parents took their places in the front row, next to Henry and Linda Bauer. Then he turned his attention to Heath and Kayla Dalton—the best man and matron of honor—walking down the aisle. Maxwell and Brenda owed them more than they'd ever be able to repay. If not for Kayla's willingness to be Rose's temporary guardian and Heath's insistence that he be Maxwell's backup, things very well could have turned out much differently. Now, the four of them were best friends, and Max had accepted a job with the Blackberry Falls Police Department.

The couple reached the front of the chapel, smiled at Maxwell and took their places—Kayla on the left and Heath on the right, beside Max.

"I've seen your bride and your daughter. Brenda is radiant, and Rose is beaming," Heath whispered. "You are a fortunate man."

"God has blessed me more than I ever could have dreamed."

The music stopped, and after a slight pause,

the wedding march began. The two people who completed his life stepped into the doorway. Brenda took his breath away. She wore a blush pink gown fit for a queen, her hair pulled back on the sides and a crystal tiara on her head. Tears moistened his eyes.

"Daddy!" Rose, wearing a white princess gown and a matching tiara, pulled free from Brenda's hold and flew down the aisle toward him. The white basket in her right hand bouncing as she ran, rose petals scattering in her wake.

Kneeling, he opened his arms wide. She barreled into him. "Daddy!"

He gave her a tight hug. "I love you, Rose."

"I love you, Daddy."

He pulled back, took her hand and twirled her around. "You...look...beautiful, princess."

"Thank you." She scrunched her shoulders and beamed at him. "Mommy's pretty, too."

Maxwell scooped his daughter into his arms and stood, her arm looped around his neck. Then he turned and watched the love of his life glide down the aisle to them—a smile on her face with enough voltage to light up an entire city.

"It seems your daughter forgot she was supposed to walk with you down the aisle." Maxwell smiled at his bride.

"*Our* daughter is simply excited her mommy

is marrying her new daddy." Brenda chuckled. "And so am I. I love you."

"I love you, too." Forgetting for a second where they were, he leaned forward and kissed her, Rose giggling softly.

"Ahem." The minister cleared his throat. "Let us begin."

Brenda turned and gave her bouquet to Kayla, and Maxwell passed Rose to Heath. Then he extended his elbow to his beautiful bride. She placed her hand into the crook of his arm, and together, they turned to face the minister.

"Dearly beloved, today we are gathered to witness the joining of…"

Thank You, Lord, for not forsaking me in my darkest hour and for blessing me with a love I never imagined. I will treasure this gift for all the days of my life.

* * * * *

*If you liked this story from Rhonda Starnes,
check out her previous
Love Inspired Suspense books:*

Rocky Mountain Revenge
Perilous Wilderness Escape
Tracked Through the Mountain
Abducted at Christmas
Uncovering Colorado Secrets
Cold Case Mountain Murder
Smoky Mountain Escape
In a Killer's Crosshairs

Available now from Love Inspired Suspense!

*Find more great reads at
www.LoveInspired.com.*

Dear Reader,

When Brenda appeared in Smoky Mountain Escape, I knew she and her newborn daughter would have to have their own happily-ever-after. So writing this story gave me great joy, and I hope you enjoyed reading it as much as I enjoyed writing it.

Brenda and Maxwell both learned the hard way that sometimes in life people will disappoint you. We cannot control what others do, but we can control our response. And we should always keep our focus on the One who will never disappoint us or leave us. When we walk with God and put our trust in Him alone, we can be assured everything will work out, even if it's not the way we thought it should.

I would love to hear from you. Please connect with me at www.rhondastarnes.com and follow me on Facebook @authorrhondastarnes.

All my best,
Rhonda Starnes

Get up to 4 Free Books!

We'll send you 2 free books from each series you try PLUS a free Mystery Gift.

FREE Value Over **$25**

Both the **Love Inspired®** and **Love Inspired® Suspense** series feature compelling novels filled with inspirational romance, faith, forgiveness and hope.

YES! Please send me 2 FREE novels from the Love Inspired or Love Inspired Suspense series and my FREE gift (gift is worth about $10 retail). After receiving them, if I don't wish to receive any more books, I can return the shipping statement marked "cancel." If I don't cancel, I will receive 6 brand-new Love Inspired Larger-Print books or Love Inspired Suspense Larger-Print books every month and be billed just $7.19 each in the U.S. or $7.99 each in Canada. That is a savings of 20% off the cover price. It's quite a bargain! Shipping and handling is just 50¢ per book in the U.S. and $1.25 per book in Canada.* I understand that accepting the 2 free books and gift places me under no obligation to buy anything. I can always return a shipment and cancel at any time by calling the number below. The free books and gift are mine to keep no matter what I decide.

Choose one: ☐ **Love Inspired Larger-Print** (122/322 BPA G36Y) ☐ **Love Inspired Suspense Larger-Print** (107/307 BPA G36Y) ☐ **Or Try Both!** (122/322 & 107/307 BPA G36Z)

Name (please print)

Address   Apt. #

City   State/Province   Zip/Postal Code

Email: Please check this box ☐ if you would like to receive newsletters and promotional emails from Harlequin Enterprises ULC and its affiliates. You can unsubscribe anytime.

Mail to the Harlequin Reader Service:
IN U.S.A.: P.O. Box 1341, Buffalo, NY 14240-8531
IN CANADA: P.O. Box 603, Fort Erie, Ontario L2A 5X3

Want to explore our other series or interested in ebooks? Visit www.ReaderService.com or call 1-800-873-8635.

---

*Terms and prices subject to change without notice. Prices do not include sales taxes, which will be charged (if applicable) based on your state or country of residence. Canadian residents will be charged applicable taxes. Offer not valid in Quebec. This offer is limited to one order per household. Books received may not be as shown. Not valid for current subscribers to the Love Inspired or Love Inspired Suspense series. All orders subject to approval. Credit or debit balances in a customer's account(s) may be offset by any other outstanding balance owed by or to the customer. Please allow 4 to 6 weeks for delivery. Offer available while quantities last.

Your Privacy—Your information is being collected by Harlequin Enterprises ULC, operating as Harlequin Reader Service. For a complete summary of the information we collect, how we use this information and to whom it is disclosed, please visit our privacy notice located at https://corporate.harlequin.com/privacy-notice. Notice to California Residents – Under California law, you have specific rights to control and access your data. For more information on these rights and how to exercise them, visit https://corporate.harlequin.com/california-privacy. For additional information for residents of other U.S. states that provide their residents with certain rights with respect to personal data, visit https://corporate.harlequin.com/other-state-residents-privacy-rights/.

LIRLIS25